DAVID WHELAN

Three Kings

DAVID WHELAN

Copyright © 2015 David Whelan

All rights reserved.

ISBN: 1503205207
ISBN-13: 978-1503205208

DEDICATION

For Alison and Josh

And all of the hardworking, undervalued people within the police forces across the country that work tirelessly to keep the streets safe for our children.

The fight will be long, but we will win one day!

ACKNOWLEDGMENTS

There are perhaps more people to thank this time around. Unlike my other books, I've had this one proof read by a few people to try an capture any mistakes, ambiguities, and mistakes that can crop up when writing.

Georgina Handley, Ian Ferguson, Tim Whelan. All of them have spent time reading this, and offering their opinions, criticisms, advice and above all encouragement. Should this be the book that makes me a million, I'll buy you something nice.

And then there is Alison and Josh.
A big thank you to them for being there for me, making me laugh and showing me support and love, despite my sometimes grumpy days.

PROLOGUE
Summer, 1984

The evening sun was falling on the long grass and the gentle breeze was brushing against the stalks. Hidden among the reeds, Patrick lay on a blanket with Georgina beside him.

They both looked at the blue sky above them, the splashes of soft clouds rolling over them. Neither had moved for nearly an hour, and Patrick himself had almost fallen asleep. The day had passed too quickly for him, as were all the days. Soon he would be heading off to university, and although he was excited at the new adventure that lay ahead of him, he didn't want the remaining days to end.

"I'll miss you." Georgina said, squeezing him softly as she lay her head on his chest.

Patrick would miss her too, he had told her before, but

for some reason he couldn't bring himself to say it to her now. He merely returned the gesture and squeezed her hand.

In the distance, above the rustling of the grass, he could hear the shouts, chatter and excited squeals of his younger siblings and their friends. He had been asked, as the eldest, to look after them and make sure none of them got hurt. He wasn't in the mood to play babysitter, having made the arrangements to spend the afternoon with Georgina, and as soon as the group had reached the river and the sandy, silty embankment, Patrick had stood over the assembled youngsters and in no uncertain terms told them to behave and look after each other.

It had worked well, he thought. He could hear the laughter and the shouts, and he managed to become attuned to the pitch of the cries so as to know when someone was seriously hurt.

There were no major injuries yet.

"I was thinking," Georgina said, "about us." She sat up and looked at him, and Patrick smiled as her soft, long curly auburn hair fell over her shoulders. "I want to give you something before you leave for university. Something you'll remember me by. Something I've been wanting to give you for a while now."

Patrick leaned up onto his elbows and looked at her. "You don't have to give me anything. Just spending time together is enough."

"I want to give more."

Slowly she leaned forward and kissed him on the lips. There was a growing sensation within him as their lips touched. It wasn't like the other times they had kissed, this moment had more feeling, was stronger and more intense. As they kissed and their tongues touched, Patrick knew he was in love with her.

Georgina pulled back from him and sat up. There was a smile on her face, a playful look as she began to unbutton her shirt. Patrick's eyes grew wide as he watched her and as she exposed her bra, he stroked her arm and pulled her close to him.

"I want to give you my body." She said as she positioned herself on top of him.

Their kisses were ferocious in their passion. The excitement was growing and the movements were becoming confused and fumbled as he struggled with the garment. Patrick had no experience of removing or unclipping a bra and Georgina pulled it off for him. There was a moment of stillness as he looked at her naked chest, and they kissed once more, his hands holding and cupping her breasts.

Their breathing was frantic, their movements becoming more controlled as they urged each other to steal the other's virginity.

Patrick was kissing her neck, his hands running down her naked back, following the line of her spine. He savoured the moment, the sensation. His senses were alive as his mind remembered each passing second. The smell of her hair, the smoothness of her skin, the whispering of his name, the shouting of his name.

From across the field, the calls of his name were hoarse and frantic. Quickly Patrick sat up and looked out towards the group by the river.

He saw his brother, Daniel shouting to him and

running towards them. Quickly Georgina pulled her shirt back on and was partly dressed as Daniel collapsed into the small clearing they had made.

"It's Jimmy. He's hurt Katie." Daniel panted, quickly spying the naked flesh of Georgina.

What was she doing? He thought. *Why was she partly naked? With Patrick, his brother?*

The questions ran through his mind as quick as Patrick was on his feet and running down to the river. Daniel was a second behind him, as he cast a scowl of disappointment at Georgina.

Patrick's lungs were burning as he sprinted towards the river bank. As he approached he saw the other youngsters, crowded around a figure, partially submerged in the flowing water. Without a second thought, Patrick jumped into the water and waded across towards the group.

As he approached he saw that Katie was seated in the water, against the roots of a partially submerged tree. Her lips were turning blue and were quivering, and given the shock of the cold water on his own body, he couldn't imagine how cold Katie was. The boys next to her parted and allowed Patrick to get to her.

"She's tied up." One of the boys said.

Patrick squatted down and looked into the scared frightened face of Katie. "It's going to be okay," he said, "you hear me Katie, everything's going to be okay." He turned to the nearest boy, Declan, and asked where James, his brother, was.

"I don't know Paddy," Declan said, his own voice shaking with fear. "We turned around and saw him with her, as we came over, he got out of the water and ran off."

Patrick cursed and turned back to Katie, again reassuring her. "Danny?" he shouted. "Give me a hand."

He looked over and saw Georgina sitting on the bank with the remaining girls, as they cried into her arms. They caught each other eyes, and the passing look passed the message that the girls shouldn't be there should the worse happen. Georgina nodded and began to gather the girls' things together.

Daniel was next to Patrick and they started to feel around the roots, trying to visualise where the ropes used to tie Katie to them went. Patrick could feel the knot in his hand and he started to run his fingers over it. Looking down through the flowing water he tried to see the knot, trying to decipher the route of the rope. He could feel his fingers getting numb from the cold, and looking at Katie, he could see her lips changing colour more quickly and her face draining of blood.

"KATIE!" Patrick shouted, trying to stir her from unconsciousness, "Stay with me Katie!"

Patrick looked at Daniel who was also frantically pulling at the rope. "Help me." He said as he pulled hard on a root within the water.

How could Daniel let this happen? He thought. He was meant to be watching them. He had delegated the responsibility to his middle brother because of the constant bickering between them. Daniel had insisted he was old enough to look after himself and the others. Patrick had relented and allowed him to stay with the group, and at the time he knew it would play well for himself as it would allow more time with Georgina.

But now, given where they were, he regretted his decision to let Daniel be in charge. He couldn't be trusted, and once more Patrick knew he had been proven right.

As he grappled with the slippery root, he felt it give a little and he fell back into the river as Daniel waded around through the fast flowing water to help.

Helping his brother back to his feet, the brothers began to pull hard at the root, using their combined strength to pull the root free. Their muscles ached and the pain shot through their arms as the root slowly came loose. Patrick held onto the root as Daniel dived under the water and began to pull the ropes down over the root, trying to give any slack possible to them around Katie's body.

Feeling the ropes around her body loosen slightly, Patrick pulled her arms free. Limply they floated in the water and he saw her head fall forward, dunking her head into the river.

"Hold her head." Patrick said as he moved back to the knot and started to manipulate it again with the extra slack.

The seconds and minutes passed like hours and the brothers continued to work to release Katie from the water as the children on the bank cried and sobbed, watching them frantically help Katie.

Patrick looked down through the water and saw a crimson blemish in the water flow from his fingers. The blood from his fingers didn't stop him pulling at the rope and slowly untying the knot.

With each movement of the rope, he felt a renewed energy pulse through him. The movements were slow at first, but as the rope gave way, they increased in speed and finally the cold body of Katie was released from the submerged roots and fell into Daniel's arms. Patrick helped his brother to the bank and as they pulled the girl onto the grass and started to cover her with blankets, he looked up to see his and the parents of the other youngsters come running towards them.

Katie's parents fell to her side and were calling her name as the ambulance crew also arrived and knelt beside her. They began to check her breathing and pulse and put a mask over her face. The other parents ran to their respective child and hugged them, pulling them away from the river and from the ambulance crew.

Daniel and Patrick fell back on the grass as Georgina fell to her knees next to them. She hugged Patrick and kissed him hard on the face.

Patrick looked up and saw the dominant balding figure of his father stand over them, and the smaller squat frame of his mother almost jump on her sons.

"Where's Jimmy?" she asked.

Both Daniel and Patrick shook their heads. "We don't know ma'." Daniel replied.

Their father was about to ask them again just as Katie coughed and was rolled onto her side by the ambulance crew. Water erupted from her mouth and she coughed again.

There was a visible sense of relief on all those present as they saw Katie open her eyes and her parents kissed her. Neither the ambulance crew, the youngsters, or any of the parents looked at Patrick King or his family as they followed the stretcher back towards the waiting ambulance leaving the two drenched brothers sitting on the grass with their parents.

Finally, his father looked down at his two sons, drenched and soaking wet.

"Find your brother." He said. "Find your brother before they do. There'll be hell to pay for this."

To some people the house would be described as cosy; to others, compact or small. But for the King Family, it was home. The familiar flagstone floor welcomed them each day and the open fire in the living room warmed their hearts, and dried their tears as whatever problems the family faced were discussed and sorted.

However, there were days when no home comforts could hide or solve the turmoil they faced. Patrick and Daniel sat together in their bedroom, hearing the shouting coming from downstairs as their father was confronted by Katie's father and a police constable. They obviously wanted to know where James was, but none of the family, Patrick and Daniel included, knew where he could be.

At least that was the official line they were telling their parents.

Being the younger brother, James had grown up in the shadows of his older brothers and as such had strived to find his own place in the family and the village. It wasn't the first time he had got into trouble and ran away, but it was the first time the police had been involved.

Patrick, being the elder brother had always strived to protect his siblings. From the time when he was at school he had taken the punishments for the fights they started in the playground; to the times their father returned home drunk when they were younger and would take out his frustrations on each of them and their mother. Patrick had tried on those occasions to stand up him to stop any harm coming to Daniel and especially James, who being 4 years younger was more susceptible to the beatings.

Sitting on the bed Patrick looked at Daniel. Despite only being two years younger, Daniel was as tall and broader than himself. An ideal rugby player, Patrick thought. If only Daniel had carried on at school, he could've made the county team and maybe be on his way to better things.

Daniel caught him looking at him. "You think he's at the abbey?" he asked in an almost whisper.

Patrick nodded. "He always heads there."

The abbey, part of an old monastery, had been used by practicing and retired priests, and monks for nearly 150 years. The local school children would always be taken there for days out each summer, and Patrick remembered the fascination James had had of seeing the monks silently, and diligently going about their daily business. There was an aura of security there, a place to feel safe with a guaranteed warm welcome from the clergy.

James, since his first visit had often sneaked off to the abbey to sit with the monks during their prayers, and on occasion he had joined them for their meals. When he had run away before, the Abbey was the first place Patrick and Daniel searched for him, and true to form, he was always there.

Ordinarily they would've told their parents where he was, but with the severity of the punishment that could be bestowed on him, both brothers decided to keep quiet.

For the time being.

"We'll go and look for him later." Patrick said, careful not to speak too loud for fear of his voice travelling to their parents downstairs. "He's safe at the moment."

It had been a long day and Patrick lay down on his bed and stared at the ceiling. His mind began to retrace the day's events.

The cold water.

The panic of seeing Katie.

The frantic moments to free her.

"What happened?" He asked. He heard Daniel shuffle on his bed, but he didn't look over to him.

Daniel closed his eyes tightly as he recounted the events. "They were playing." He said. "As we always have done, swinging out over the river. I went to get a drink, and I don't know – James and Katie must've headed further upstream. I didn't see what happened until Declan came running over."

"You were meant to be in charge of them." Patrick said.

Daniel looked over at his brother, and saw the look on his face, the one that mirrored their mother when she disapproved of what they had done. He was about to argue with Patrick, counter the accusation that he had failed in his duty of care and state that Patrick himself had also failed. But he was too tired to argue. He knew his brother would try to find a way on the superior moral high ground, trying to be the mature son in the family to win over the grace and blessing of their father. He opened his mouth to protest, but he couldn't find the energy. "I did my best." He said simply as he lay back on the bed.

Patrick lay silently for a moment and remembered the look of fear on Georgina's face.

Georgina.

The touch of her skin, the warmth of her body the memory of her was etched into his senses. He could still smell her perfume wrapped and embedded in his hair and breathed deeply to savour the rich sensual memory.

Patrick closed his eyes and started to think over those moments with her. He could still feel the kisses on his lips, and the feel of her naked flesh. He started to smile but then opened his eyes to see Daniel looking at him.

"What?"

Daniel said nothing as he lay back on his bed and looked up at the ceiling. The arguing voices from downstairs were muffled and difficult to make out and he tried to block out the sound as he rolled onto his side, away from Patrick.

Georgina.

How could she be with Patrick? He thought. She was his age, not Patrick's. They had grown up together, had played together as children, they had stolen each other's first kiss when they were 13.

What was she doing with Patrick?

He remembered walking with her to school, and how they had walked home hand in hand. He smiled as he remembered that tender moment of young teenagers, the anxiety he had felt and the doubts of whether he should or shouldn't touch her hand.

Thankfully she allowed him to take her hand and they walked the 3 miles home together, smiling at each other.

When they had finished school, Daniel had gained a place at a college in the larger town, while Georgina had been pressurised by her family to stay in the village to help on the farm. They still saw each other, but not as often as they used to, and with each passing day he could feel that they were drifting apart.

He knew they would never be able to rekindle those precious moments of their early teens, but he at least wanted to know there maybe could've been the possibility of it. Seeing her part-naked body, with Patrick though had hit him hard. Now all the chaos of the events at the river and Katie were starting to ease back, his mind thought back to the moment he had disturbed them.

He had no idea Georgina was with him. Daniel had invited her to come with them, but she had declined saying she had other plans. But she was there, with *him*.

His mind started to think about the meanings behind her actions, trying to formulate a pattern, an explanation for what he had seen.

She declined him, but accepted his brothers invitation. Why? Was it a sudden acceptance? Not likely – the manner in which she was undressed suggested she was comfortable in his presence, and for that it takes time.

He knew they were friends, but he had no idea they were that familiar with each other. Patrick was about to go to University and Daniel was studying for his higher exams and being at a college in the local town meant he wasn't around the village as much as he used to.

Was that his window of opportunity? Was that how she had come to be with him?

He and Georgina had vowed to be friends for life, and he had no doubt that that would happen, but deep down within his soul he knew he wanted more to come of his friendship with her. He loved her, his heart and head knew that.

His feelings for her had grown over the years and he was waiting for the moment to tell her. He had it all planned out ready, on the day he would be accepted into the police force, he would tell her his true feelings. But now, how could he do that if she was with Patrick? She wouldn't hold the same feeling back to him, despite all the times she said she cared for him.

He could feel a bitter taste in his mouth. Adrenaline. His heart was pumping fast and he could feel the anger build up within him. He wanted to lash out at someone, but he knew he had to keep control.

How dare she! He thought. *How dare she betray me!*

The house was quiet and Daniel was woken by the gentle shaking of his shoulder by Patrick. Wearily he sat up and saw it was 2 a.m.

"They should all be asleep." Patrick whispered as he pulled his coat on and carefully opened the door.

The brothers headed downstairs and with each careful step they stopped to listen for any sign of life in the house. Only the gentle crackle of the dying logs on the fire could be heard.

They had trodden the boards before over the years, as they had sneaked out to meet friends, or sneaking back in

14

after staying out longer than they promised they would. They knew the boards that squeaked, and which ones would take their weight to allow a stealthy path.

As they carefully stepped across the floor, there was a movement to their side and the brothers turned to see their father sat in the chair next to the dying fire.

"I wondered when you two would go and get him." He said, his voice just above a whisper. He nodded for them to sit down, and feeling like children being caught in the biscuit cupboard, they sat on the low, spring ridden sofa.

Their father had worked in the fields around the village all of his life, and had either a personal or professional relationship with everyone within a 10 mile radius. He had grown up with the villagers, got drunk with the local police officers, and over the past few hours he had tried to pull every favour he could to protect his youngest son. But the young girls family were pushing for James to be arrested and questioned about his actions. They were calling it attempted murder and were pressurising the police to charge him. But first they had to find him.

He looked at his sons with a tired, pleading look they had never seen in his eyes before. Yes, he had mistreated them over the years, he knew that, but they were still his sons, and while he wouldn't admit that he loved them, he did.

He regretted the way he had treated them, the guilt plagued him for days and weeks, and he knew the guilt forced him to drink, and the drink caused him to act upon his children in a manner no father should.

It was why he stopped drinking five years previously,

and looking at those years, the best five years of his marriage and life.

But with the stress of the day, he had opened the remaining bottle of scotch and poured himself a glass. He could see his sons nervously looking at him and then the drink.

"I haven't drunk any." He said to them as he leaned forward. "Look, you know as well as I do where he is. He's at the Abbey. What I want you to do is-"

"We'll bring him back." Patrick said quietly, interrupting.

His father shook his head slowly. "No," he said. "Don't bring him back. I want you to speak to the Abbot, or at least ask someone to take this to him." He handed Patrick an envelope, bulging with paper inside.

"There's a note in there," their father explained, "A doctors letter explaining Jimmy's behaviour, and the medication he needs for his schizophrenia. There's also money. I want the Abbey to protect Jimmy, to look after him for the foreseeable future. He wants to join them anyway doesn't he? Why not send him there a year or two early, at least he'll be safe there."

Patrick took the letter and turned it over in his hands. Questions ran through his mind. *Why? How could he? Does mother know?*

A thousand questions, but he couldn't form one of them in his throat. He hoped Daniel would be able to speak, but from the look on his face, he too was as dumbstruck as he felt.

"I need you to do this." Their father said. "If he comes back here, he'll be strung up. Tell the Abbott or whoever you speak to, I'll make financial contributions to his education and wellbeing. It's for his own good."

Patrick and Daniel nodded and both silently stood up. Their father had made a decision and they had to abide with it no matter how much they disagreed. They turned from him and left the house without another word being spoken.

PART ONE

LUST

CHAPTER 1

Present Day

The music was loud, throbbing on the ears as the repetitive bass drum beat pounded the walls like a unrelenting hammer. Caroline could hear the familiar ringing in her ears, as she often did after her weekly attendance at the nightclub.

She had arrived nearly three hours before with her friends, and using their combined charms that only women have, they elegantly swept past the security guards and into the VIP section. As the group of women passed the burly men, they cast an eye at the exposed flesh each of the women were showing. Be it legs, chest, midriff or back, the guards nodded their approval at the young women as they entered the fabled VIP lounge.

The champagne quickly flowed and the women were starting to relax into their plush surroundings. The large sofas cushioned their landing as they fell giddily onto it, laughing like children who had just found their parents drinks cabinet.

The VIP lounge overlooked the main dance floor and the soundproof windows shielded some of the music. The dark dance floor below them looked ethereal as the lights flashed and the writhing bodies of the partygoers were illuminated for a split second.

Caroline and her friends swayed and moved to the music and the drinks continued to flow.

She had caught his eye first.

Adrian had been standing at the bar with his two friends and had ordered beers. As they took their first sips, they cast an eager eye around the VIP area.

Her figure hugging dress showed not a bump out of place, and she leaned over her friends to grab the bottle of wine, the material rose up her leg, exposing more of her thigh as the fabric dropped from her body to allow a glimpse of the roundness of her breasts.

Adrian smiled to himself as he eyed his possible next sexual conquest, but not wanting to draw his predatory friends attention to his prey, he turned slightly away from her, as if to suggest he hadn't seen her.

Throughout the rest of the night, as the men circulated the room, he had kept an eye on her. Her dark hair, hanging over her shoulders, suited her, he thought. He could see her face, could see her shaped chin and soft eyes, giving a sparkle of playfulness as she looked directly at him.

Contact was made, he thought.

He watched her closely, casting a look over to her and

her friends occasionally, and he saw that she was looking back at him too. He saw they were nearing the end of their bottle of wine and indicated to his friends that he was getting another round of drinks in.

His companions were engrossed in an argument about the latest football match to notice Adrian stand at the bar with the woman.

They smiled at each other.

"That's a nice dress." He said, leaning towards her, smelling her perfume.

She smiled back at him, "Thanks, I bought it today. It was either this or nothing."

It was Adrian's turn to smile and he gave a cheeky wink. "Nothing would've got you more attention."

"But this got yours." She replied, giving him a small smile.

It was a game, he knew. A game he had played many times before, and one he had to admit he hadn't mastered yet. If he was to break the rules down, there were too many variables conflicting with each other, too many actions and reactions, too many unpredictable factors and alterable expectations he had no control over.

It could be small things such as the temperature in the room, the volume of the music, or one of her shoes rubbing her feet. For all he knew, she may have had a bad day at work and that would be effecting her mood hours later.

He could see the same woman the next night and say the same thing to her, but he may not have the same response. And the only difference may have been holding her gaze a second longer to appear too eager, or to break eye contact too soon so as to suggest he wasn't interested.

Years of practice hadn't allowed him to have a final solution to the skill of picking up women, but whatever he had done tonight, he was going to be happy with the results.

Their first kiss was on the dance floor. The bodies of the masses pressed around them, the music pounded through their heads, but there was no relenting in their embrace.

Their tongues explored each other's mouths as their hands ran over the other's body.

Caroline wished she hadn't worn her engagement ring, but it was too late now she thought, as Adrian's hands grabbed her buttocks and pulled her closer to him. Her partner wouldn't find out, she figured. Her friends were finding their own way home with Adrian's friends, why should she miss out on some much needed physical attention just because of a ring on her finger?

She pulled Adrian's head down towards her and shouted in his ear. "Let's get some air."

Adrian nodded and held her hand as Caroline headed to the emergency exit.

The cool air hit them hard and as the doors behind them closed the muffled music accompanied their frantic kissing. The alley way was devoid of anyone and they headed towards the shadows where Adrian pinned Caroline to the wall.

He kissed her neck, his hands were running over her body and squeezing her breasts. She could feel the excitement in her body grow, and, as her hands explored him, she could feel him grow too.

There was a knowing look between them and quickly separating, Caroline pulled her knickers down and Adrian unzipped his flies.

He entered her body easily and the love making was quick, in time to the rhythm of the muted dull music behind them. Caroline hoisted up her skirt and lifted her legs up around his waist as he continued to push further into her. They kissed again, mouths locked around each-others, their breathing was hard and fast and Caroline closed her eyes and enjoyed the sensation of the man inside her.

She listened as she heard the man groan and grip her body tight. He paused and stayed still, holding her against the wall. Caroline didn't want to move a muscle as she smiled to herself at what had just happened.

"That was amazing." She said, opening her eyes.

Adrian still didn't move and she pushed his head away. His body fell backwards and crumpled to the floor. Caroline stood and looked in horror at him, and then looked up to see a black clad figure holding a silver knife.

It took her mind a second to compute what had just happened, but it was too late as the figure lunged at her and impaled the knife into her body, piercing her heart. She tried to shout out, but a gloved hand grabbed her head and pulled her face into his shoulder, smothering her mouth and nose as he pushed and twisted the knife in her body.

Caroline convulsed as the knife moved and the attacker could feel her momentarily tense up as the remaining ebbs of life drained from her. Carefully he stepped back and lowered Caroline to the floor next to Adrian.

The figure looked down at his two victims and wiped the blood from his knife on the dead man's clothes. He looked around himself and checked there were no witnesses to the murders. As he thought, there were none and he calmly walked away, to the far end of the alleyway, towards the street. As he walked, he pulled a piece of paper out of his pocket and dropped it.

It had one word typed on it: LUST

CHAPTER 2

The blue flashing lights of the patrol car welcomed Detective Chief Inspector Patrick King as he walked across the road from his car. Having such an incident in a highly public area as a nightclub would obviously draw crowds, and with the drunken revellers eager to catch a glimpse of the scene, now covered with blue protective tents, he wasn't envious of the uniformed officers trying to keep order.

He remembered his own early years within the force, and how he too had had to keep the peace when confronted with an inquisitive and boisterous crowd. There was always a morbid fascination and inquisitiveness for members of the public to try and glimpse a crime scene. But from the distance they were at, behind the outer cordon tape, all they could see would be the blue tent, and maybe, if they were lucky, one of the forensics officers in their

25

white paper suit.

He entered the scene, ducking under the tape and headed towards the incident command van. Inside he saw some of his CID officers already in attendance, and with them, in their white paper suits, the Scenes of Crime Officers. He saw the Lead SOCO, Michael Ferguson. "What have we got?" Patrick asked, although he already knew part of the story, having been informed by the force control room and quickly reading the initial log on the computer.

"Two bodies," Ferguson said, reading from his notes. "A female, ID in her purse names her as Caroline Richards, aged 23. The deceased male is Adrian Leyton, aged 27. At the moment, it looks like single knife wounds to each of them, but until we strip the bodies and get them in the mortuary, we can't say for certain because of the blood."

"Do we know what they were doing there?" Patrick asked.

Ferguson smiled, "A young couple, in a nightclub. I think they were being a bit frisky. His flies are still undone, her knickers are around her left ankle. They're also not a couple." He added.

Patrick raised an eyebrow in question.

"We found a photo in her purse of herself and a male we think is her partner." Ferguson replied to the unasked question. "Not the deceased male next to her."

Patrick thought for a moment. Their reasons for being there were plausible. They now lived in a society where young people would have sex in an alleyway rather than booking a hotel room, or borrowing their parents car like he had to do back in his day.

He asked about CCTV cameras from the nightclub and was informed that officers were downloading the footage at that moment.

He had a professional team, they all knew their roles and what questions to ask. Patrick's role was more to oversee everything and ensure procedures were adhered to. He was the head of the team, head of what he saw as his *family*, and his officers all looked up to him for leadership. Every investigation had hurdles to overcome, obstacles and issues to solve. Mainly financial, Patrick thought. Despite running major murder investigations, there was always the continual battle to keep the financial cost of the investigation down. When he heard his own senior management team say to the press *"No expense will be spared to solve…"* he knew the true meaning to state: *"We'll spend as much as we dare until we know we won't be able to solve it."*.

"What do you think we can get from the bodies?" he asked Ferguson.

"The usual." He replied. "Swabs of hands and fingernails, hair combings, fibre tapings of the body. There are probably a hundred or so, probably thousands of empty beer bottles back there too. Not to mention the fag ends."

"We need them. Take them."

Ferguson had known Patrick King for a number of years, and had watched from the comfort of his own desk in the Forensics unit as the young DC King had risen up the ranks to become an Inspector. He had worked with him on a number of big cases, including the recent murder of a four year old boy in a penthouse apartment in the city centre. He respected Patrick for his dedication to the job and determination to the investigation, but he had to admit that Patrick King's knowledge of forensics was limited. "Sir, you realise that will take possibly days to collect every single item, and we have no idea how long some of them have been out there."

"They're in my crime scene," Patrick replied, "I want them."

"And submitting them?" Ferguson asked. "It'll cost a fortune." He had had a similar discussion with other officers who had asked for a substantial amount of work and manpower from the SOCO team, which in return had yielded little to no results with none of the exhibits being submitted for analysis and subsequently left to rot in an exhibit store for the rest of time. He was determined not to waste his or his team's efforts on a task that would take them nowhere.

"Just get them will you?" Patrick said, his voice suddenly becoming more serious, heavy with authority.

Reluctantly Ferguson agreed to the request. There were times when he would've stood his ground and refused, but he could sense this wasn't one of them. He made a note on his pad to add the task to collect and seize all the bottles and cigarette ends from the scene, but he added it at the bottom of the list.

Patrick listened to the other snippets of information that had been gathered in the short space of time since the incident had happened, and he could feel an almost tingle of excitement within him. Depending on the results of the forensic tests, the whole investigation could rely on old fashioned police work, he thought. Interviews, witness statements, and trawling through hours of CCTV footage from the street and the nightclub, to try and find any clue to the identity of the assailant.

There was a lady in the corner of the cabin who caught Patrick's eye. "What's your role?" he asked.

"Public relations," she replied. "We need a media statement."

The media.

Patrick tried to hide his dissatisfaction at the mention of them. They were a thorn in the side of any major investigation, with their sometimes intrusive questions and thirst for any information.

Despite having a family member working within the press, he had had too many arguments about the role of the press and the conflict it had on the official role of the police.

He saw them as an accepted devil within society. People he knew had a right to know the basic details, especially in this case where, what could be a total stranger, attacked a young couple. At the moment they had no idea what sort of offender they were dealing with, and he preferred to keep the details of the case as far from the prying eyes of the press as possible.

"Okay," he said, "but it's basic information only. We'll give them the facts, the spiel about pressing forward and finding the culprit, no expense spared and all that. But if they start asking in depth questions, you stop it and get me out of there."

*

The snort of the coffee machine as it frothed the milk barged through his head like a pneumatic drill. Daniel King closed his eyes as he waited for his cappuccino to be served to him in the cardboard cup.

He paid for his drink and filling it up with five sugars he pushed his way through the commuter crowd and out onto the street.

The early morning rush for the city workers was well under way, and Daniel forced his way forward, trying not to spill his drink.

In his pocket his phone rang. Readjusting his shoulder bag he pulled it out and answered it. It was Colin Parker, his news editor.

"Where are you?" Parker asked abruptly.

"Station Street, I'm minutes from the office." Daniel replied, stepping to the side to allow the pedestrians to hurry past him.

"Don't bother coming straight in. Head to police headquarters."

Daniel took a sip of his drink but stopped as he heard the instruction. "What's happened?"

"A double murder." Parker said. *"There's a briefing at 10am. I want you there."*

It took a moment for his mind to try and comprehend the reasoning behind the order. *A double murder?* That would mean his elder brother Patrick would be involved in the investigation. *Would he be leading it? Was that why he was being sent to the briefing?* If he was totally honest, attending a police briefing would be a more constructive use of his time, given the meeting with senior members of the corporate board he had later that morning.

"I'll be there," he said after a moment's silence. "But I'll be late for that other meeting."

Daniel could hear Parker sigh down the phone at him.

"I know. But I want you there. I'll hold off the bosses here for you for as long as I can, but I want you there, and I need you to work your magic. You understand what I mean don't you?"

Daniel forced a grimace as he listened to his editor. He knew exactly what he meant, but he couldn't help but find the hypocrisy and irony of being asked to try and garner unpublished confidential information from his brother, when the very meeting he was risking being late for was to discuss those very actions at the cost of losing his job.

"Yeah, I know exactly what you mean." He said before hanging up.

Work his magic. Daniel thought.

Would he be thanked for it? Would he be rewarded for getting an exclusive report for his paper? He doubted it very much. He knew the senior managers were out to get him. He had brought embarrassment and turmoil to the desk of the owner of his newspaper, Marcus Book.

Critical insubordination and rueful neglect of duties was the over inflated and ridiculously worded accusations against him. He was only doing his job, as he was requested to do now, to get any information from unofficial sources within the police, no matter what the price was.

So he had. He had paid off police officers for snippets of information into the current police investigations and he had written up the stories. But when the public outcry of the abhorrent callousness of the newspapers tactics was too much to bear, the newspapers owners circled the wagons and went on the defensive.

It was during the initial stages of the *scandal* when Daniel worked on another story that he uncovered evidence of Marcus Book's son being arrested on suspicion of delivering and distributing Class A drugs. Somehow though, the young Calum Book was released without charge and many believed it was due to his father's influence.

No, he thought. It wasn't going to be the best meeting to attend, and he thanked Parker for the opportunity to try and avoid the meeting.

The room used for the briefing was the same as he had visited before, Daniel noted. At the front was the long table, lined with microphones and recording devices. The backdrop was the standard police poster-stand, emblazoned with the crest of the force and the banner-line of *"Protect the community, Serve all"*.

Inappropriate wording, Daniel thought.

Where were the police to protect the victims of this murder?

He knew the police had a difficult role and he understood that in real terms there was no way they could be everywhere all the time to stop every crime. But he could also see the stupidity in the *power phrases* that adorned the police banners. The public relations department was obviously well paid that day, he mused as he shuffled to the side and leaned against the wall, or more likely he thought, the PR guru's had been on a corporate image and style writing course. *How much of the tax payers money had been wasted on that?* he thought.

All of the chairs were occupied and Daniel was forced to stand. He nodded to a few of the other reporters he recognised from other briefings, and from those few unofficial meetings where information was shared.

He also nodded and smiled at the blonde female

reporter in the second row, Sally. He had spent an unofficial evening and night with her, without his wife's knowledge. She brushed her hair back over her face and seeing Daniel standing at the side of the room, she turned away from him.

Daniel smiled to himself at her reaction as he finished his drink and threw the cup into the bin.

At the front of the room, the doors opened and a high ranking police officer stepped out in front of the cameras, a flurry of flashes illuminated his every move. Behind him were two more officers, the last to appear was his brother, Patrick.

The room calmed down as Detective Chief Superintendent Whithers began his briefing.

"At approximately 4am this morning, the police resource team received an anonymous phone call relaying information that two bodies were located at the rear of The Crossed Keys Nightclub." DCS Withers said. "Officers were dispatched and upon attendance, they located two persons lying in the alleyway to the rear of the night club. Emergency resuscitation was commenced, and emergency response teams were requested. The ambulance crews who attended pronounced life extinct at the scene for both victims."

He paused and the silence in the room was exponentially overcome by the shouts of questions from the media. Daniel didn't raise his hand, he didn't shout out a question. He had been to these briefings before and he knew that the officers would only give as much information as they were willing to give. No matter how a reporter twisted, or over complicated their questions with double negatives and oppositional statements. He knew the officers would stick rigidly to the party line agreed behind the scenes.

"At this time," Withers said, "I'd like to pass over to Detective Chief Inspector King, who will be spearheading this investigation."

Spearheading? Daniel thought. Management speech to make it sound like they were hunters.

Patrick took a sip from his glass and straightened his tie.

"Ladies and gentlemen," he said, a slight crack in his voice Daniel noted. Was it nerves? "At this moment we are in the early stages of the investigation into this double murder. I will not be revealing the names of the deceased until we have spoken to their families, and offered them our full support. Nor will I be confirming the circumstances of their deaths. In addition, I will not be surmising, hypothesising or guessing at the identity of the offender or offenders.

"What I can say is that at the moment we have 25 dedicated officers working on the case, and that doesn't include the uniformed officers at the scene, the forensics, the search teams, and the other backroom staff. We have leads, and are investigating them. The post mortems of the deceased will take place within the next couple of days."

Daniel made a few notes on his pad, but as his brother rounded off his prepared speech, he headed towards the exit, leaving the rest of the media pack to shout their questions at Patrick, only to be met with silence from the officers.

CHAPTER 3

He knew he should quit, but there was no feeling like a cigarette. His wife had pestered him for years to give up, and after working his way through patches, pills, and even hypnotherapy sessions, he still craved a decent cigarette. Finally it took the look and honest words of his daughter, Clarissa, "Daddy, if you don't quit, you'll die.", to convince him he should smoke his last one and throw the pack away.

Patrick promised he would, but added the provision that should stress at work take its toll, he would be allowed one cigarette only.

Clarissa agreed.

As he headed from the press conference, Patrick could feel the need for nicotine to coursing through his veins and as he headed down the stairs to the smoking shelter, his hands flexed in tension.

With the shelter in view, Patrick rummaged through his pockets but swore when he couldn't find his cigarette or lighter.

Not now, he thought. There had to be one somewhere.

From his side, the other smoker in the shelter tapped him on the shoulder and handed him a cigarette, and taking it with almost shaking hands he accepted the lighter too.

The first breath of the toxic smoke electrified his nerves and he thanked the other smoker.

"Don't mention it big brother." Daniel said.

Patrick looked up and coughed as he saw his brother standing before him. "What the hell are you doing here?"

Daniel casually blew smoke up towards the concave plastic roof. "I was asked to cover your briefing."

"I know." Patrick snapped. "I saw you. But I want to know what you're doing here now?"

Daniel indicated the cigarette in his hand. "For a detective you're not very observant are you?"

Patrick shook his head and took another toxic breath. "That's why I have a team of people working for me."

There was a moment of silence between them.

It had been a few months since they had seen each other, and then they had parted on difficult terms. Patrick had contacted Daniel to try and stop his newspaper from printing reports of corruption within the police service. He didn't want to do it, but he was asked, no, he corrected himself, he was ordered to make the request by his superiors. They thought that having a family connection would make it easier to stop the publishing of the story, but instead it had only made the editors print it a day early.

In their eyes, the fact that Patrick had tried to stop it, meant there was some truth in the allegations. And, as a thanks to the confirmation from the top brass, the editors decided to leave Patrick King's name out of the paper when they also reported that a senior officer had tried to bully the paper into silence.

A moral stance against corruption, the paper had said it was.

Patrick was a hairs breadth from losing his job, and he swore never to be put in such a situation again. He was determined to be more careful who he spoke to, what information to divulge and never to trust a reporter, even if it was his own brother.

He never blamed Daniel for the actions of the newspaper, he knew he was merely a journalist trying to do his job, and would be under instructions, like he himself was, to try and get more information from Patrick.

"You going to ask me anything?" Patrick said.

Daniel gave a sly smile. "Would you tell me anything?"

"No."

"Then why should I ask?"

Patrick stubbed the remainder of the cigarette out under his shoe. He really needed to quit, he thought. That had made him feel sick.

Daniel watched him and just as his brother was about to leave without another word he spoke. "Do you think it was a stranger attack or the young lady's boyfriend in a frenzied attack?"

Patrick turned back to him. "I didn't say -"

"You didn't have to." Daniel said, interrupting. "Two

people, to the rear of a club, of course they'll be up to no good, shagging. But I'm going to guess it was a stranger attack, but being you, and being as careful as you are, you're not going to admit that in there."

There were a thousand things, he wanted to say to him, but Patrick instead held his tongue and chose his words carefully. "So what do you think happened, being the big shot reporter?"

"I've been to these things before. I've heard a hundred officers, like you just now, describe a hundred murders. I've also seen the end results of the investigation, and I've seen the correlation between the first briefing notes and final suspect in court."

"What are you getting at Danny?"

Daniel stubbed his own cigarette out and stepped forward, facing his brother. "You didn't use the word *frenzy*, or *savage*, or any other word that describes the ferocity of the murders. They may have missed it in there, but I think, based on your statement, that it wasn't a frenzied attack. If it was, you would've said so to conjure up images of a crazy killer on the streets. It also would've meant the boyfriend in a fit of jealousy seeing his missus being banged up a back alley by some bloke she's just met in the club, would've done it. The briefing was refined, almost sterile. You don't know who it was, and you think it was a stranger."

Patrick stood still for a moment. Given all of his vices, all of the difficulties Daniel had caused him over the years, with his gambling and drink addiction, there was no denying his brothers aptitude and skill into reading between the lines in a situation.

He often thought that his skills would be of better use

within the police, but being stubborn, he knew Daniel always preferred to be a thorn in Patrick's side. And given his current role as a reporter, was a big enough thorn.

"An interesting theory." Patrick said. "But you're wrong."

"So it is the boyfriend?"

"I didn't say that either." Patrick said, knowing he had just side stepped a trap. "What I mean is, I didn't use those words because out of respect for the deceased, and their families, I don't want to cause them anymore upset by going on TV and telling the country that their loved ones were butchered -"

"They were butchered?"

"- or died of single stab wounds." Patrick said, ignoring the interruption. "Look, I have to get back." He walked out of the shelter and turned back to his brother. "Have you decided on Christmas yet? Georgina asked me again this morning."

Daniel remembered the text message he received a few days previously asking if was going to join them for Christmas lunch. With everything going on at the newspaper, he hadn't replied. "I don't know." He said. "Probably. When do you need to know by?"

"As soon as." Patrick said. He paused for a moment, and it was obvious he was thinking about asking something else. "Are you going tomorrow? To dad's grave?" he said finally.

"Yeah." Daniel said, his mood no longer that of a reporter. He pulled his coat close to him. "Will James be there?"

Patrick shrugged. "No idea. I guess so."

"Do you still have dad's watch?"

Patrick pulled his sleeve up to reveal the silver watch, leather strap and roman numerals on the face. "Wear it every day."

"It's a nice watch."

Patrick agreed and a silence fell between them once more. A difficult wall that stopped them talking to each other. With nothing more to say, he turned from his brother and left him alone in the smoking shed.

As he watched Patrick walk away, Daniel pulled his notepad from his pocket and turned to the pages of notes he made during the briefing. He wrote on the paper, *STRANGER, SINGLE STAB WOUNDS.*

As much as he loved his brother, he had to admit he was always a terrible liar, and with his adding the *single stab wounds* comment, it was too specific to be anything more than true.

At least he had something more than the other reporters, he thought.

As for meeting Patrick at the grave, Daniel stared out at the wall across the car park. He didn't want to go, but it was the anniversary of their father's death, he felt a duty to be there. His own relationship with his father hadn't ended well, and Daniel hadn't been there like Patrick or James in the final days as the lung cancer finally destroyed him, but he had managed to find the strength to attend the funeral, and he remembered that whilst sitting in the chapel, listening to James give the eulogy that he started to feel the guilt for not seeing his father one last time.

He remembered how his mother had passed Patrick their father's watch during the funeral service, from father to son. His father had passed it on to the son who had been most loyal, Daniel thought. There was no way he would ever be his father's favourite, and he decided then that he promised to attend the grave each anniversary, if he could.

The incident room in the Investigation Team's office was a hive of activity. Patrick entered and saw his junior officers on phones, discussing the case and calling across the room to others.

He wondered as he walked through the melee of activity and entered his office at the far end if any progress had been made. There was a window of opportunity in any murder investigation where the offender could be identified and found. They needed an idea of who the murderer was within the first 24 hours, or their chances of solving the crime would diminish. As the hours and days would pass, he knew the correlation of finding the murderer would diminish and lessen. He therefore needed to make sure his officers were always working a lead on the case. If a question raised another 10 questions, you answered all of them, and if those questions raised another 10, you stayed until they were answered too.

In his mind he ran through the list of objectives he hoped his team had addressed.

Had the CCTV been checked?

Had the witnesses been interviewed? Had the doormen?

Had the relatives been informed and were they receiving the appropriate support from the Family Liaison officer?

What about the boyfriend of Caroline Richards? Had

he been questioned? Could this be the work of a revenge attack from a jealous boyfriend?

He was mulling over the questions when his office door opened and DS Helen Kolar and DC Keith Brookes entered.

"Where are we with things?" Patrick asked.

Helen answered, running a hand through her shoulder length dark red hair. "It's not the boyfriend." She said bluntly. "He works for the Ambulance service and was at a job on the other side of the city."

"Is that how he found out?" Patrick asked. "He heard it called in?"

"He heard there was a stabbing," Brookes said, "but the name of the girl wasn't divulged over the ambo airwaves."

"It would've been a crappy way to find out." Patrick said. He almost felt disappointed. In cases such as these, there was always a good chance the offender would be the partner. "What about ex-boyfriends? Partners? What about Adrian's partners and girlfriends?"

"We're checking." Brookes said.

"Check quicker." Patrick snapped.

"We are but -"

"What?! But what?"

Brookes looked at Sergeant Kolar, almost for support. "We don't think the offender was known to the victims. It wasn't a frenzied attack."

Patrick stared at the Constable as he spoke; the summation of his brother spinning through his head. Daniel had guessed right and in doing so, Patrick had inadvertently given him more information about the case.

"Check again." Patrick said. "Check every statement, every line of enquiry. Then check again. If a question raises a dozen routes of enquiry, then check every one!"

"But-" Brookes was cut off.

"But nothing. Just do it. Do your job!" Patrick snapped.

DC Brookes left the office, casting a quick glance at Kolar as he left. She caught his eye and nodded to him, as if to say she agreed with his objections, but it was best to simply do as he was told.

Alone in the office, Helen Kolar closed the door and turned to her superior.

"Don't do that!" she said. "Don't shout at this team, my team, and don't do it when other people can hear you. It demoralizes the team and none of them will trust you or your judgment."

"I don't need -"

"And don't you dare speak to me in that way!" she added, interrupting him. "Don't think that you can speak to me in such a way and think I'll continue to share my bed with you."

Patrick sat in his chair and looked at Helen.

He recalled their first time together; a team drinks night out where the alcohol flowed freely, and by the end their hands were just as freely exploring each other.

The desire to lay his hands on her, and lay her on a bed had been growing within him since she had transferred to his team six months before. He had caught her eye a number of times, and he could see there was a reflected desire of emotion from her to him. That night out had been the perfect catalyst for their desires to be tipped over the edge. Neither of them resisted the others advances and as the drunken mob of their colleagues continued on their course towards the next bar. Patrick and Helen stayed behind the group, and in the back of a taxi their first kisses were exchanged. That night had ended well for both of them, exhausted and their skin glistening with sweat.

That was four months ago, and while Patrick had found the first lie to his wife difficult, he had found the strength to continue to deceive her. Being in his position, it wasn't uncommon for him to work late into the night, and this offered the perfect opportunity to find a few precious hours in the arms of Helen.

He liked her. More than he promised himself he should or would like her when their affair had started. It was her self-assured confidence that he found appealing. The manner she would stand up to him, as she just had, in private and in front of the troops.

She was a good officer, he knew. He had heard her name mentioned in meetings before she joined his team, and her reputation for being an effective and team driven Sergeant was well founded. Her assertiveness in team meetings, and her willingness to stand up to her superiors had made it somewhat easier to have a secret life with her. There didn't need to be pretending or over-the-top behaviour to counteract any overt signals they thought might be given off to the rest of the team. Their behaviour and formality in each-others company would be seen as a power struggle between the two officers, and not as it was, pent up, hidden sexual tension.

He liked her a lot.

"I saw my brother." He said finally.

Helen sat down opposite him. She had heard of the difficulties they had had, not just from the newspapers and other media outlets, but from the general rumour mill the police service offered. "Did you speak to him?"

"Briefly." He said, "Don't worry," he added seeing the look on her face, "I didn't give him anything, and he knows better than to ask." He lied.

He ran his hand through his hair and scratched his head. "I don't want to mess this one up."

Helen leaned forward, her demeanour becoming more considerate and caring, like a lover. "You won't. It's not you against the world, we're all here doing the same job. It's a team effort. I'm here for you too."

He looked up into her blue eyes. "Can I come over to yours tonight?"

She smiled at him and stood up, "I've never said no so far.". Helen winked at him and left the office.

For a moment, Patrick sat in his chair and thought about Daniel, the way he had surmised, guessed and correctly predicted the nature of the killer.

He really should've been a copper, he thought as he stood up and looked out at his team of officers working. Would their relationship have been better over the years if they had worked together?

He had sometimes thought why Daniel hadn't joined the police too. He remembered the way he would talk for hours, constantly about the police, reading hundreds of books, watching TV shows. Daniel knew police procedures at the age of 13 better than some officers Patrick worked with now, he thought.

What had changed his mind? Why didn't Daniel work

harder and join the force, he could easily have made the rank of Sergeant by now. Perhaps, Patrick thought, Daniel's marriage wouldn't have broken down if he had a more suitable career.

Patrick didn't totally disapprove of Daniel being a journalist. He knew he was good at it, he had proved his ability to sniff out a story time and again. There were times when he had put his innate investigative ability to good use, uncovering child pornography rings, a scandal of sexual abuse in Westminster, or the issue surrounding the son of a media mogul who had been caught trying to sell drugs.

But then, as had been proved, his investigations could cause Patrick a world of trouble. Corruption in the police had been unfortunately common place for a number of years. Wealthy politicians, businessmen, and criminals would always find an officer eager to earn more money in exchange for intelligence and information, or for deleting records from the computer systems.

He didn't know how Daniel had managed to find out, but he had published a story of a Chief Superintendent who was in the pocket of an underworld crime boss. The only way the information could've come about was either through the police or the criminal fraternity, and given the harsh, brutal and sadistic punishments the gangsters dispensed, there was no way anyone from that world would've spoken to the press.

That left the police, and that led to internal investigations and exposed dozens of examples of unauthorised press relationships with the police.

The investigation had easily made the link between Patrick and Daniel, and as such the finger of suspicion fell on him. But no proof was ever found that he had passed on the information. Instead, he was ordered by the senior officers to approach Daniel and ask him to have his newspaper cease publishing the damning stories about the police and the leaks.

But it didn't work.

Unbeknown to both Daniel and Patrick, the newspaper management of a rival newspaper had a private investigator follow them and record and document the meeting. The following day, the photos of the Detective Chief Inspector and his reporter brother were published, *proving* who was responsible for the betrayal within the police.

Patrick was summoned to a disciplinary hearing and the accusations thrown at him. He had strongly defended himself, stating he was sent at the request of the senior management. But there was nothing he could do to persuade them and when it appeared that Patrick was about to lose his job, the then Deputy Chief Constable intervened and unofficially confirmed Patrick's statement.

He was cleared of any wrong doing, but to make it appear as if the police were conducting themselves properly, Patrick was reprimanded. But unofficially, he was given the opportunity to continue his work on the Major Crime Team.

How ironic, he thought, that the police cover up the resolution of an investigation into corruption.

Patrick shook his head as he remembered the turmoil it had brought him and his family.

Would Daniel have been more trouble in the police? He thought. *Better the devil you know!*

At least as a reporter, he could keep him at arm's length.

CHAPTER 4

The news room was alive with activity. Daniel loved the feeling and adrenaline rush he got from entering the heart of the newspaper and knowing there was an impending deadline.

He loved the fact that each day, they started with a blank piece of paper, and throughout the day, each man and woman would work solidly, researching, writing, editing and checking all the information they had gathered, ready for the editors approval and subsequent printing.

Daniel was a more senior journalist, and enjoyed the few perks that came with it. The slightly larger desk, a more comfortable chair. He tossed his bag on his desk and turned to his colleague, Ryan. "How are things looking?"

"Page one is this double murder." His colleague

replied, glancing up at Daniel occasionally, but not breaking his typing speed. "I think the Boss is holding a quarter of a page for you, we've got art of the crime scene, a few decent snaps of the police tent and a bobby on the scene tape."

Daniel nodded and looked at his watch. "Where is he? Parker?"

"In his office I think."

Daniel started to tie and tidy his neck tie. "I have a meeting with him and the executives. Can you start the basics for me and I'll polish it later?"

Ryan stopped typing and looked at him. "You want me to do your work?"

Daniel smiled and patted him on the shoulder. "Is that OK?"

Ryan shrugged off the hand and turned back to his computer. "Leave your notes, I'll only do the basic outline for the copy."

Daniel thanked him and headed towards Colin Parker's office. He was met by an empty room and he turned back to the bullpen. "Anyone seen Parker?"

The conference room was glass lined onto the corridor, and through the breaks in the slanted blinds, Daniel could see the suited executives seated around the table. Some he recognised, others he didn't. He caught the eye of Colin Parker who met him at the door, taking him aside into the corridor.

"A few more people there than we thought." Daniel said.

Colin shook his head and shot a glance back towards the room. Daniel could see he was stressed, the lines on his face were more pronounced than normal, and despite the man's 6ft height, and heavy girth, his body seemed to be slumped and almost trying to shrink away from a world that had recently dealt him nothing but body blows and heart ache. "They've brought lawyers down."

"Lawyers? What the hell?" Daniel said, trying to cast a look into the room.

Colin held up his hand to try and calm Daniel. "I know, I've already had a massive bust up with them already. Look, Danny, I need you to keep your cool in there. They will try to rattle you, but you need to keep your head."

"I will."

"Danny?"

"I will!"

"Daniel? You hear me? If you lose it in there, I can't protect you. You'll be out of here quicker than shit off a stick."

"Then let's see how far they can fling me." Daniel replied as they entered the conference room.

He felt like a child.

In fact, from the way they were talking to him, Daniel was being treated like one too. It was evident that the senior management and lawyers had no idea about the time sensitivity of the world they lived in. They had strict deadlines, and while all workers in offices across the world have deadlines, more often than not, theirs could be moved and delayed.

Journalists had a deadline they *had* to meet, otherwise, there would be no newspaper the following day., and if there was no newspaper, then they wouldn't make money.

Perhaps he should put it to them in those terms, Daniel thought. It's the only way management will listen, when there's money at stake.

He bit his lip, refraining from saying anything as he checked his watch again. They had sat in the meeting for over an hour, and it was an hour that the news-floor needed their editor, not having him tied up in such a meeting.

But, Daniel had to be subjected to the snide, skittish idiocy of the lawyers before him.

They're all the same, he thought.

Throughout his divorce, every conversation with solicitors and subsequent barristers were like banging his head against the wall. They were all the same, each one thriving on the last minute rush and desperation to prepare for a case.

Despite his own solicitor taking enough money off him each month to barely leave him a few pounds to live on, Daniel had expected him to have some sort of knowledge of the case before entering the family court to ask for duel custody of his daughter. But no. With seconds to spare, he sat on a bench watching as his solicitors frantically read through the files once more.

"What's the name of the girl again?" the solicitor asked.

"Louise, Louy." Daniel had replied, exasperated. "Shouldn't you know this already?"

The solicitor ignored him as he scribbled her name on his yellow pad and then looked up at Daniel. "Let's get in there then."

Daniel had followed him into the court, his confidence in his solicitor hitting a new low. He was right to be nervous, as they emerged half an hour later being granted only two weekends a month to see Louy.

He detested solicitors and lawyers, controlling people's lives by their own limited interest in the case at hand.

His thoughts were brought back to the conference room as he heard his name repeated once more. He turned to the man asking him the question, an executive within the parent company of the newspaper, Richard Evans.

"What was the question?" Daniel asked absently.

Evans looked at him over the top of his glasses. "I said, do you think it's appropriate for a person within this organisation to publicly criticise the owner of the newspaper he works for?"

Daniel paused for a moment and looked around the table, watching each man as they waited for his answer. "No." he said simply.

Evans raised his eyebrows and cocked his head, expecting a more worthy answer. "Would you like to explain? Or perhaps to expand your answer."

Daniel leaned forward, took a sip of water from his glass and looked at Evans. "No." He said calmly. "I would not like to explain or expand my answer."

Evans took his glasses off and rubbed his eyes. He was tired and frustrated with the lack of response from Daniel King. He had a job to do and he needed answers to take back to his own senior managers, and then they too to Marcus Book, the owner of *City Times News*.

"I have a job to do." Evans said. "I need to gather information, to find out in what circumstances the criticisms of Mr. Book and his company were given, and what else you may have shared with rivals to embarrass him, his family, this newspaper, and *Persephone Enterprises.*"

Daniel leaned forward. "I've explained all of that already. I've written a formal statement, I've answered emails, and all of the questions you've asked me. I'm not stupid, I know that the comments I made embarrassed him. But, if we were to listen to a transcript of this entire meeting, we would not hear anyone deny that what I said was untrue, a lie, or factually incorrect." He looked around the table at them all, and he noticed the shuffles in the seats, the movements, the glances to each other. He had hit a collective raw nerve, and their silence had done more damage to their own cause by inadvertently confirming his assumption, than someone trying to deny it. Daniel knew he was right, and he knew they agreed with him.

"And what," Evans asked, "do you say about the accusations that you passed information to police officers, and they passed details of their investigations to you?"

Colin leaned forward and placed a hand on Daniels arm to stop him speaking. "We've covered this already."

"I want to hear it again."

"Why?" Colin asked. "His answer won't and hasn't changed."

"Did you receive details of a police investigation from any member of the police force?"

"This meeting has finished." Colin said, pushing his chair back and signalling for Daniel to move.

"We're still talking." Evans said, standing also.

"Then you guys stay here and talk," Colin said, "we're going back to work."

"Marcus Book will hear of this." Evans said forcefully.

"Then tell him." Colin retorted. "Bring him down

here, tell him to bring his sorry ass down here. If he's going to fire me, tell him to do it in person. But I'll tell you now, I'll tell all of you now, so sit there listen up and make notes. If he fires me, I'm taking half of that news room with me and we'll walk straight into the offices of his rivals and we'll put on their desks every single rumour, gossip, scandal, and humiliating story we know about him and throw it back in his face. I will make it my mission in life to destroy him and his reputation."

"You shouldn't make idle threats." Evans said coolly.

Colin stared at the man. "I've been a reporter and worked in the media for 28 years. I've worked in radio, newspapers and commercial television. I've had three divorces, two heart attacks, and the only way you will destroy me is with kryptonite." He looked at the men around the table, boys more like, he thought. He watched as none of them held his gaze. "Tell him what you want, but don't you dare think you can walk in here and bully me, or a member of my staff. Don't take me on! Marcus Book may own this newspaper, but I run it."

Silence fell on the conference room and Colin was the first to move turning from the table and ushered Daniel out.

They were in the elevator heading back to the news room when Daniel finally spoke. "Can I say, that I think I was the calmest person in that meeting."

Colin gave a small smile. "Don't rest Danny. They'll come back with their knives sharpened and aiming at both of our hearts. The only thing to protect us is the success of the paper." He looked at Daniel. "If you lied about getting information from the police or not in there, I don't care.

But I need you to work your magic and get me the best story you can for these murders. Do whatever you need to do. We need to show them the results of how we do our job, we need to show them that they need us to be a success more than we need them. Do whatever you need to."

Daniel nodded in understanding and stood in silence as the elevator descended.

PART TWO

SLOTH

Chapter 5

The nights were getting colder, he could almost smell it. The air was different, the winds were picking up, and the autumn aromas were giving way to the harsh winter. His ragged clothes were more than well worn, and well stained.

Another trip to the clothing bank, he thought.

His shoes were worn thin and the laces had snapped so many times that he no longer bothered to try and repair them. With unwashed, scraggy hair, a dirty beard and sunken eyes, Leo pulled his aching knees up to his chest and tried to stop the constant shaking.

How could his life have spun out of control, he thought.

Too many years had passed, but he could remember the days of heading home from work, unlocking his front door and kissing his wife. He remembered how his son would run into the kitchen and hold onto his leg and pull him towards the living room to play.

They were magical memories and as he sat shivering in the cold, his mind quickly retraced the steps he had trodden to begin his downfall to the gutter.

It started at an office party. Leo and his colleagues had gone out drinking, and with sufficient alcohol infesting their body's and brains, they returned to their office late into the night to continue the drinking. As vodka shots were poured from the secret stash hidden at the back of a filing drawer, someone produced a small packet of white powder.

They were jubilant and excited at the prosperous deal they had just cemented, and they knew congratulatory letters and a bonus payment was on its way to them.

The owner of the powder sat at the desk and carefully cut the powder into relative equal lines. One of the men bent down and breathed a line of powder up his nose and fell back, rubbing his nostril, as the powder worked its way into his blood stream.

Each man took his turn and then they turned to Leo. He tried to refuse at first, but the baying calls of the alpha males forced him to inhale the drugs.

The hit was immediate and he felt the effects course through his body at lightning speed. He fell against the wall, knocking folders and papers to the floor, and grabbed onto the nearest chair, slumping into it.

His head spun as the drugs worked their magic, and after the initial shock to his system, he felt the euphoria begin to build up within him. He had never felt anything like it and as the feeling began to wear off some hours later, he was eager to try it again.

During the following days, the supplier from his office refused, claiming he didn't know what Leo was on about. As the days slowly ebbed by, his need for that sudden rush of euphoria was greater than he could've possibly known. He was itching for some of the drugs again. He couldn't sleep, he couldn't concentrate, he was desperate for something to take him to that angelic high once more. But the more he asked his colleague, the more he was rebutted until one day the man subtly suggested where he might be able to obtain some.

It hadn't taken Leo long before he had his own drug underworld contact, and he was buying a gram of narcotics a day.

However he soon found himself asking for more, withdrawing more money from his personal bank account to fund his habit, and then he used the joint account with his wife to pay his dealer. The few thousand pounds worth of savings was soon used up and Leo had to find other means of paying his debts.

He was involved in the monetary transfers of large sums of money between the parent company he worked at and the company's subsidiaries and professional partnerships. It was all creative accountancy, he thought. A few hundred pounds of missing revenue wouldn't be missed if he syphoned it off every few months. He started to transfer small amounts of funds from the company accounts to a small holding account in the name of a made up business he inputted onto the database. It was through this new account that he withdrew his spending money.

On a Wednesday morning he was called to his

mangers office and the evidence of his theft of company money was laid down in front of him. He tried to dispute the facts, but he couldn't and when he refused to take a drug test, he was summarily sacked from his job and given half an hour to pack his desk.

He walked the shameful mile from his desk to the elevator in silence, watched by his colleagues, including the man who had introduced him to the white cobra that had poisoned his life. Flanked by security guards he was escorted from the building.

As his car pulled up onto the driveway, his only thought was for a shot of powder to steady his nerves, and as he entered his house, he confessed his actions to his devastated wife.

The following months were a blur as he was forced to move out of the house, the divorce was quickly signed and he was given no access to his children. Finding a shabby cheap hostel to live in he tried to find work, but the other drunken and drug fuelled residents dragged him further down into despair and soon the low paid work he had managed to find excused him of his work. But he didn't care, he only wanted the drugs.

The alcohol was enough to ease the need for the narcotics and as the days passed, he found himself drinking more and more. Sometimes he wouldn't be able to find his way to the shelter or the hostel and he slept on park benches.

He had soon become one of the very people he had ignored as he walked to work in his fresh suit. He looked up at the office workers and begged for money, reaching out to them, pleading for any coins they could spare, but he was met with looks of disgust and contempt.

He looked at his dirty hands and remembered the day he realised he would never again feel like a man, and he started to cry.

Leo hadn't heard the footsteps, and as he opened his eyes, his drunken mind struggled to make out the shape that was crouching beside him. In the confusion of Leo's mind he tried to form an answer to whatever question the man had asked him, and he mumbled what he thought was a coherent response.

He went to lie his head back on his cardboard pillow when the man spoke to him again.

Why wouldn't he just go? Leo thought.

He was someone to be ignored, not spoken to. It had been too long for him to remember how to interact with someone when they offered a kind word. He looked up at the figure and swore at him.

Within a second Leo was grabbed and a fist hit him hard in the face. He was too drunk to react with any effort and the punches continued to rain down on him.

He instinctively pulled his arms to his head, legs pulled to his chest and he curled up into a ball. The man continued to hit him and then, as suddenly as it had started, the attack ceased.

Leo waited a couple of seconds, trying to listen for any movement of his attacker, and then finally he moved his arms and looked out into the alleyway.

The man was gone.

With pain racing through his hands, arms, legs and head Leo moved out from under the makeshift shelter and crawled out into the puddles. There were other homeless people around, each as destitute and unwelcome as he was, but there was no sign of movement from any of them.

Was it a figment of his imagination?

He reached up to touch his bruised face, just as a kick caught him in the chest and he heard a rib crack.

In pain and gasping for breath, Leo tried to call for help, but the man was on top of him, pinning him down. Leo tried to reach up and fend off the attacker, but his brain couldn't co-ordinate his arms properly and the man soon subdued him.

Leo looked up into the man's face, covered with a hood. He could make out vague details, but nothing that stood out as specific. He was about to shout again when he felt the sudden pain in his chest.

He looked down and saw the handle of a knife protruding from his body, the man's hand gripping the handle firmly. Leo tried to move, but his strength was seeping out from him too quickly and soon he closed his eyes for the last time.

The man took a breath and stood up, wiping the blade of his knife on the clothing of the tramp. He looked down at the body and calmed his breathing before turning from the dead body and walked away.

As he walked he pulled a piece of paper from his pocket, on which was typed: SLOTH.

CHAPTER 6

James King loved the early mornings.

Despite not sleeping well, he climbed out of bed and dressed in silence, washing himself at the sink that stood in the corner of his room. Mindful not to wake the other residents of the parochial house, he headed downstairs to the living room.

It wasn't necessarily his role, but he still found himself each morning lighting the open log fire and then boiling the kettle for the morning drinks.

As the fire flickered into life, James followed the white washed corridor, passing painted memorials of saints and religious imagery. At the end of the corridor was a large wooden door. He pushed it open and entered the vestry. Passing through another set of double doors, he entered the large sanctuary of St Mark's Church.

Silence met him as he walked across the carpeted path towards the altar. Steps led up from the nave towards the main altar with the intricate reredos looming high above him, reaching up towards the domed ceiling. The reredos was an altar piece, sculpted and carved from differing materials and adorned with images of religious iconography.

James could see the central figures of Jesus Christ, and to his side, Mary his mother and St Peter. Each time he looked up at the gilded piece of work, he marvelled at the craftsmanship that went into it.

As he crossed the central line of the sanctuary, he genuflected, and crossed himself, whispering a quiet prayer to himself as he kissed the gold crucifix that hung around his neck.

He found himself a seat at the end of front pews and sat and watched as the morning sunshine began to rise through the stained glass windows and bathe him in a kaleidoscope of colours. As he watched the sun rays fall across the altar he closed his eyes and allowed his mind to relax.

It was a ritual he completed each day. He used the peacefulness of the chapel to try and focus his mind. Ever since those first visits to the Abbey as a child he had found solace in the comfort of sitting before the altar of Christ. It wasn't perhaps a surprise to himself then, maybe more for his family, that he followed a path into the church and took his vows of service as a priest before his 22nd birthday.

It was a proud day, when his family attended his ordination as a priest. He remembered how focused his mind was as he lay prone, face down on the floor, before the steps to the altar as the Bishop read out the blessings and vows that he would forever uphold and would forever believe in. He made a promise to God that day that he would be as good as he could be; he promised not to judge or to criticise; he promised to help and support where he could, advise and guide those persons who asked for it.

He smiled to himself as he remembered the joyous looks on his parent's faces. Looks of pride. And he fondly remembered how his brothers looked on in almost awe as he was accepted into the clergy, and his position within the church was confirmed.

He heard the muted footsteps to his side and opened his eyes to see a young priest approach him with a cup.

"I've brought you some tea." The young priest, Fr. Martin, said.

James accepted the drink and invited him to sit with him for a moment.

"Thank you for the offer," Martin said. "But I wish to study for a while before the day starts properly."

James smiled and nodded and allowed Martin to head back to the parochial house. He watched the young man go, and admired his dedication to his studies. It was a different time now, he thought, from when he had chosen to become a priest. There wasn't as severe a stigma on a young man in his day if he chose the path of clergy as there was today.

He understood why though. With the global church embroiled in scandals and criticism for some of its views, which contradict the accepted liberal social attitudes of the world, James knew it would now take a more dedicated and devout man to accept the strict rules and responsibilities of being a priest, when all his friends would be drinking and searching for their next sexual conquest. It takes stamina and a great deal of self-control to become a priest, and he hoped that Martin would continue with his studies and achieve great things.

Confident he was alone once more, James pulled a small bottle from his pocket and unscrewing the top he poured two tablets into his palm. Pocketing the bottle once more he looked at the tablets. He hated taking them, but it was a necessary evil he told himself. He needed to control his symptoms and the painful headaches that accompanied them. When he had attended his recent appointment at the hospital with Daniel for support, the doctor increased his dosage. It was stronger than what his body was used to, and there were other side effects to them, but the hope was his body would adjust to the drugs and medication and his symptoms would be controlled more effectively for the foreseeable future.

It wasn't against his vows to take prescribed medication, but there was a part of him that felt ashamed of them. His Archbishop in the Diocese was aware of his condition and had supported James throughout his dark days as the symptoms took their toll on him. But other than Archbishop Kennedy and Daniel King, nobody, not even the young priests he lived with, were truly aware of the dramatic effect his condition could have on him.

Swallowing the tablets, he checked his watch and saw it was nearing 6am.

James bowed his head and recited a prayer asking for the guidance of God to help him conduct his duties in the manner expected of him, he crossed himself and headed back to the house.

"Bless me Father, for I have sinned." The voice behind the black veil and mesh in the wall said quietly. *"It's been a month since my last confession."*

James sat quietly in the dim light and waited as the lady in the confessional box began to speak. He had always been fascinated by the notion of the Sacrament of Confession, always been interested that people would confess their perceived sins to a man who they believed represented God.

Ironic, he thought, *that fallible men should be the early representative of an infallible God.*

There was no denying the Catholic Church had had too many scandals over the years. With stories of abuse, embezzlement, illicit affairs, pregnancy and drug use all happening within the sacred walls of the Church, how could the clergy be sure that their sins were being forgiven, if the man they are confessing to could be holding sins on his soul that far outweigh the penitent.

It's the way it is. He told himself. Those people seeking confession needed something to believe in. They need a guide to follow, and if he, a secretively cracked and tarnished priest could be that guide for their soul and beliefs, then so be it. James believed in the teaching of the Church, and he sought to bring those teachings to the masses. He wasn't going to denounce the sacrament of confession, given all of its obvious flaws. He had taken an oath and he was going to fulfil it to the best of his ability, with no judgement of those who seek his forgiveness.

"I have been a difficult wife to be with." The lady said from behind the curtain in the confessional. *"My husband, you see, he's had some bad news from the doctor and his knees are getting stiff*

in the winter. I've tried to be supportive, and I'll always do things for him, but, Father, there reaches a point where I snapped at him the other day. I know he suffers and I know it's his illness, but I just snapped at him. I'm a bad wife."

James knew the voice of the woman, she was one of the cleaners who volunteered to clean the church every day. He knew about her husband and how she was struggling with him, she would tell him, Martin, and the other volunteers at any opportunity she could get. She wanted support, she needed help, and as if he could, James wanted to try and give her that.

"It's a normal reaction," he said softly. "You're behaviour is a normal reaction to an unnatural situation. Sit with your husband and tell him what you feel. Apologise to him, and he will forgive you."

"Thank you Father."

"Recite two Hail Mary's and the Our Father."

"Yes Father."

James prompted the lady to begin reciting the 'Act of Contrition' and as she concluded, he said a quick prayer. "I absolve you from your sins."

"Thank you Father."

"God bless you, go in peace."

He listened as the lady left the confessional booth, and then checked his watch. It was nearing midday. He crossed himself and exited the confessional seeing there were no other parishioners wishing to confess their sins.

Maybe they hadn't sinned, he thought, or more likely, the people were becoming less inclined to confess their sins when there were so many sins in the world already.

He hoped it was the first option, as he headed back

towards the altar.

*

The alarm chirped and wearily, Patrick rolled over and pushed the button to switch it off. His body and mind needed another few hours rest, but he knew he wouldn't be allowed that luxury.

With difficulty he pulled the sheets off him and rolled out of bed and automatically headed to the bathroom. Switching the shower on, he stood at the sink as the steam started to fill the room. He wiped the mirror clean and saw his weary, tired features staring back him.

It had been a long night, he remembered. He hadn't got home and into bed with his wife until 3am, and now, having only 3 and a half hours sleep, he was starting to feel the effects. He stared at himself in the mirror and thought back to the previous evening and started to regret spending those few precious hours with Helen Kolar. He couldn't make his mind up what he regretted more; not taking her up on her offer to stay the night, or being there and making love to her in the first place.

He was the first to admit it was ironic that while he was unfaithful to his loving wife, he would always try to end the night in bed with her. His misplaced loyalty and dishonesty, he had told himself.

Patrick entered the kitchen and felt the kettle, checking if it was still warm. Satisfied it was he made himself a coffee and turned to see his wife Georgina at the table.

"You were late in last night." She said, sipping her

own drink.

Patrick tested his own drink, allowing himself to formulate the lie in his mind. "Sorry, it was manic. We finally managed to get the CCTV footage and there were a couple of other leads we needed to check."

Georgina looked at him, "I wasn't asking for an explanation. I know you have a job to do. I was just saying."

Patrick tried to hold a neutral look on his face. Had he just given too much information? Had he over compensated with his deception? He knew he couldn't dwell on it too long.

"I'll try to phone tonight if I'm going to be late." He said, in an effort to pacify her.

Georgina didn't say anything else, he didn't know if she truly believed him or not. It wasn't the first time he had been late home. She understood that his position and job required him to stay over at short notice. But there was something there in her look, he thought, or was it his own guilt making him see things in her behaviour and words that weren't really there? He quickly decided on the latter and tried to focus. But there were questions running through his mind.

Had she called the office and tried to speak to him when in fact he had gone home with Helen?

Did she suspect him of infidelity?

Was her calm persona a ploy to force his guilt to burst forth and make him confess?

There were a thousand questions racing through his mind, but he knew he couldn't let them dominate his thoughts. He needed clarity and patience if he was to continue his deception.

"Are you going to your father's grave today?" she asked.

Patrick took a quick breath as the conversation changed topic. "Yes. I'm meeting James there at 11."

"And Daniel?"

Patrick shrugged. "I saw him yesterday, he said he would be there, but you know what he's like. He could be, he may be, but he probably won't."

"I need to get changed." She said as she placed her cup and cereal bowl into the sink, kissed Patrick on the cheek, and headed back upstairs.

Patrick watched her go and felt the relief fall upon him. He loved his wife, he loved his family and his children and he worked hard to give them a decent standard of living. But he was quickly reaching the point where he couldn't continue the lie, and he knew he would have to make a decision between Georgina and Helen.

Whatever happened, he knew he would hurt one of them. He understood the old adage of *the grass is always greener* was true when it came to physical sexual relationships.

He enjoyed the love making with Helen, she was confident and knew what she wanted in bed. But Georgina was his wife, he loved her and she had stood by him through his difficult times. Would Helen do that for him? Would Helen be a capable step-mother to his two children? Would she want to be a step-mother?

They were questions he was nowhere near asking her, and if he was truly honest, he was nowhere near ready to start thinking that way.

As he stood alone in the kitchen his mobile phone vibrated and he answered it.

"Gaffer," the voice on the phone said. *"We've got another body."*

CHAPTER 7

The grass was freshly cut and as Patrick walked towards the grave, he saw the cuttings stick to his shoes. He tried to kick them off, but soon gave up as he would only have to repeat it all when he returned to the car.

The cemetery was quiet with only the distant noise of the road heard over the chirping of the birds. It was a strange place to feel inner peace he thought as he walked past the rows of headstones carved with the names of the deceased.

He read their names and ages as he passed them. He made an effort to walk a different route to the grave on each visit and to read the names on the headstones, as if allowing the names to be recognised, and to show the souls in heaven that the names hadn't been forgotten.

Ahead of him, he saw a man standing at the grave side, and from the long black coat, with his head bowed, he knew it was James.

He stood back for a moment as he watched his youngest brother say a prayer over the resting places of their parents and when he made the sign of the cross, Patrick quietly whispered "Amen."

He turned to Patrick. "I didn't think you'd come."

Patrick stepped forward and laid the small bunch of flowers at the base of the headstone. "Things got hectic at work. But I promised I would always be here."

"Have you seen Daniel?"

Patrick nodded. "I saw him earlier. He was at the briefing I gave."

"Paddy," James said his voice almost full of frustration, "You shouldn't give him anything. You've too much to lose."

"It was an open briefing. He got the same amount of information the other reporters got."

James didn't look convinced. He knew how well Daniel's analytical mind could read the truth from within a web of lies. "Just be sure you did." He said. "I don't want you going through the same as last time."

"Can we not talk about work please?" Patrick said. He didn't want to be reminded about the career turmoil he had faced, and even though he knew James was just trying to help and protect him, there was something about hearing it mentioned by his brother. It made it more personal, as if it unknowingly hurt his family more than he realised.

"I'm just saying -" James started to say.

"I know, but I've a lot going on and I can't allow myself to think about that now." Patrick almost snapped. "I vowed never to give any reporter anything, no matter who they are." He added quietly.

James knew the scandal involving Patrick and newspapers was still emotionally raw for his brother, and he could see the stressful effect it had on him, and on his home life. It was unfortunate Daniel was also involved in the scandal, and their conflict of professional interests had spilled over into their already fragile brotherly relationship.

James had tried to be a mediator between them both and had listened with the ear of a priest to both sides of their arguments, how they felt about each other, and the others actions. He had never wanted to take sides and his advice to them both was the same: *Talk to each other,* he had told them, and would continue to do so.

James was a firm believer that communication and talking were the key to smoothing rifts and arguments, but he found it difficult to get his elder siblings to sit down and discuss it without it descending into another heated squabble.

But he knew they were as stubborn as each other and such advice would be ignored and for almost a year he had seen his brothers drift further apart, further than they already were.

It was however poignant, he thought, that it was the death of their father, three years to the day, that had brought them together once more. The three brothers had stood at the side of the grave, staring at the mound of earth piled on the coffin of their late father, entombed with their mother who had passed away 11 years earlier.

James remembered how he had stood at the side, his bible in his hand and rosary in the other. He had allowed another priest to conduct the funeral mass, but had conducted the final committal to the earth of his father's body himself.

The three sons had stood at the graveside, each of them lost in their thoughts and memories, the other mourners had slowly left them alone, passing words of condolence to them until they were alone.

To his surprise, Daniel had spoken first, simply offering to buy them both a drink. It was a small gesture, but one, James saw as major step forward for them both.

As he stood near enough in the same position now he felt the urge to ask about their relationship, but he knew it was firstly the wrong time and place to ask, and Patrick wasn't one for commenting on his feelings.

They stood in silence for a moment longer and both turned to see Daniel approaching.

He joined them at the grave side and looked at them both. "Here again."

His brothers both gave a forced smile and then James spoke. "I think one of us should say something."

"You're God's man, be my guest."

"Danny!" Patrick snapped.

"What?" Daniel said. "Don't pretend you want to be here brother, I know you'd rather be elsewhere right now."

They both stared at each other, both wanting to say something, but to start an argument over the grave of their parents would be insensitive and a betrayal of their souls and memory. Patrick spoke, breaking the stare with Daniel.

"Carry on Jimmy."

James took a breath and opened his bible, sensing the roll of the eyes from Daniel. "Don't worry, Danny Boy," he said quietly, "this won't take long."

James was right, Daniel thought.

It didn't take long. He had long given up on believing in God, and while he accepted and to some extent admired his brother's dedication and devotion to Catholicism, Daniel could see the flaws with the teachings of the bible. He had argued with his teachers at school about the scriptures, the writings in the bible, and the fundamentals of the religion.

He remembered the reaction of his parents when he declared he wouldn't attend church anymore. His mother broke down in tears, and his father had yelled at him, demanding that he believe in God and the church. His father stood over him in the living room, pointing at his crying mother. "You see what you've done to your mother? You've broken her heart and you've thrown the teachings of God in her face!" he had shouted.

Daniel had wanted to shout back, but he knew, as Patrick and James knew too, that to antagonise their father was asking for punishment. Especially if he had had a drink. While the scars and bruises from his father's outbursts had healed, Daniel, like his brothers, still wore the emotional damage he had laid upon them.

So it was confusing and totally against his wishes, that he should even be there at his father's graveside to pay him homage. *Why should I?* he asked himself. *Where was God to protect me when that belt struck me across the back of my legs? When his fist broke my ribs?*

He had told Patrick this when he refused to attend their father's funeral, but Patrick had forcefully told him he would be attending, for all the faults their father had, he was still their father and should be treated with respect.

Those were words that set fast in Daniel's mind from that day. The way Patrick had purposely shown their fathers watch to him and almost declared that he was *"the new head of the family."*

Daniel didn't reply and turned from him, stating once more that he wouldn't step foot into a church again.

However he did.

He didn't know if was guilt or something else, but for only the second time since declaring his split from the church, he attended his father's funeral.

He recalled a sense of loneliness and how scared he was when he entered the church for the first time since his teenage years for the ordination of his brother at the cathedral. Despite his opposition to the teachings of the church, he still loved his brother, and he agreed to attend the ceremony and celebrate the occasion with his family.

He also knew what it would mean for James and his parents.

However Daniel still arrived at the last minute, taking his place on the front pew with his family just as James emerged from the sacristy, following the archbishop in the arrival procession.

He had caught James' eye and saw the joy in his younger brother's face as he saw Daniel there. He also saw the nod of approval from his father, and his attendance there smoothed the rift that had grown between them.

Then there was his father's funeral itself. There was no way he could avoid it, and he was reluctant to admit Patrick was right that he should attend and show his respect to him, but he knew his brother was correct.

He had stood mournfully looking at the coffin before the altar as the priest talked about the deeds of his father, the good work he had done, and about those he had left behind. But naturally, Daniel thought, they had left out the part of domestic abuse and violence he had rained down on them over the years.

It was an emotional day for him, and it was the first time he had spoken to Patrick properly since the media frenzy had attacked his brother with regards to his actions with the press.

As he now stood by his car waiting for his brothers to join him, he lit a cigarette and took a deep breath. He may have been a lapsed catholic, but he still understood the manners of not smoking over somebody's grave.

He watched as his brothers walked slowly towards him and he thought about how different their lives had become.

A priest.

A journalist.

A police officer.

Different paths forged into the world, each man finding their place in the society and each one having their own place and effect on the community.

They were each so different, he thought, but somehow so similar.

He knew in their own individual way, they had their own influence over the public. He, with his newspaper, could forge and mould opinions and ideas from the repetition of stories and editorials.

James could influence his congregation through his sermons and lecturing on the teachings of the bible. Patrick had power over those persons he was investigating, sometimes having their lives in his hands as he made decisions of arresting them or not.

He had seen people in similar positions to his brothers prepared to abuse the trust bestowed on them; and while he and his siblings relationships could be frayed and difficult, there was a knowledge there that they would always hear the truth from their family if it was deemed they were carrying out their duties incorrectly.

"What are you talking about?" Daniel asked as they came closer.

"Paddy was just saying he has a couple of big jobs going on." James said.

"Another murder?"

Patrick looked at his brother, eying him suspiciously. "Yes. I'm sure one of your colleagues will tell you about it."

Daniel noted the tone in his voice but ignored it. He didn't want to get into an argument with him. "I'm sure they will." He said. "Are they related?"

"Danny!" James said.

"I'm just asking."

"You're trying to get information." James said.

Daniel cast a glance at James and stubbed his cigarette out on the floor. "Some people say I'm a talented journalist." He said. "I've investigated some big stories, and uncovered massive crime syndicates, many of which the police haven't been aware of; and it was my research that brought the convictions. I think I'm fairly well placed and skilled enough to work out if these two are linked."

Patrick was about to speak and retort when James stepped in. "Well as long as your investigation doesn't interfere with the official one."

Predictable, Daniel thought. James would always try to find common ground, a halfway point for them to share whatever it was they were both doing. He had done it as a child, when they squabbled and he continued to do it now.

There was a moment's pause as the three of them stood at their cars.

"Will you be coming to Midnight Mass on Christmas Eve?" James asked Daniel.

He looked at his brother. "I doubt it. You know my feelings on the church."

"Charlie would like you to be there." Patrick said. "It's his first Christmas as an altar boy and he wants his uncle there."

Daniel almost swore, but he bit his tongue. "I'll try." he said finally, but knew his brothers took that as meaning he wouldn't be there.

James told them he had to head back to the church and bid his brothers goodbye. After he had driven off, Patrick unlocked his own car and stood at the open door.

"Danny, I can't stop you making your own enquires into these murders, in fact, I know you're itching to." he said, "But I ask you, not to make contact with me in any way with regards to them. It won't do us any good. You must have other contacts in the force, I know you shouldn't have any, but I bet you do. But please protect them."

Daniel nodded in agreement.

He did have another person he could call upon for information, and he made a mental note to contact them once he had done some of his own background checks.

He could also see that it was hard for his brother to ask that of him. Reluctantly, he reciprocated. "I will. And Paddy, if I do find anything that I think is a major lead I'll let you know. Whoever has killed these people needs to be caught, and I don't want to get in the way of justice. If I find something, I'll leave it with Jimmy."

Patrick thanked him and climbed into his car. "Join us for Christmas will you. The family all together for once."

"I'll think about it." Daniel replied smiling.

Patrick shut the door and smiled to himself, knowing that his brother would come. There was always one thing he could count on, Patrick thought, and that was the ability to persuade his brothers to do things, when it came to personal family matters. He knew it was right for the family to be together, especially at Christmas, and as the head of the family, there was no way they could counter his logic. If there was one thing his father had taught him, it was how to garner the respect of those around him.

CHAPTER 8

Patrick looked at the two pieces of paper, each individually typed with a single word: LUST and SLOTH.

The pages had been collected and seized from each of the crime scenes, and while nobody at first made the connection due to different forensic officers attending the different scenes, a chance throw away comment in an office caught the attention of someone and a connection between the crimes was made. The two pieces of evidence were brought together.

"There're no prints at all on them?" Patrick asked.

"No." DC Keith Brookes replied. "They were both pretty wet when they were recovered, the SLOTH one especially, but the Forensics Unit did all they could, chemically treating them both. But no, nothing on them."

Patrick held up the sealed evidence bags, looking at them hard, as if trying to glean more information out of the one word statements. "And what do we think about the two words? How are they connected? Other than being English?"

Brookes looked at his colleague, Andrew Chamberlain, "We're not too sure, but-"

"I swear to god," Patrick interrupted, "I'll knock heads together unless people start making educated guesses." He tossed the pages onto his desk.

"They're the same words used in the Seven Deadly Sins." Chamberlain said finally.

The office was silent as Patrick stared at his two officers.

"Seven Deadly Sins?"

"The Divine Comedy" Chamberlain said. "Story of descent through the levels of hell."

"What are the others?" Patrick asked.

"Sir?"

"What are the other sins? You said there were seven?" He repeated.

The two officers looked at each other, and Patrick quickly got up from his chair and entered the main incident room. "Can anyone tell me the Seven Deadly Sins please?"

He was met with silence. "Anyone? Can anyone remember their own collar numbers?"

There was more silence. "Well I'm glad to be working with such a knowledgeable group of educated fools." Patrick said.

"Greed, gluttony, envy, pride, wrath, sloth and lust." A lone voice called out from the rear of the room. Patrick looked over to the officer who called out and saw a young uniformed officer sat at one of the desks.

"Who are you?"

"PC Neill, sir." He said nervously, "I just came up for a word with Daz Thompson."

Patrick smiled at the young officer. "You're not going anywhere, you're joining this investigation." He turned back to the room. "OK, listen up, as crazy as it seems, this is the best idea we've had so far. It shows the murders are possibly linked, so start to go through the personal histories of the victims, try to find out everything. Find out the life of this homeless man and see if he could've had any contact with the first two."

He faced Chamberlain and Brookes. "Good work you two. Have a two minute break."

They both smiled at the Chief Inspector and headed back to their desks feeling invigorated by taking the investigation forward a step.

Patrick entered his office again and was met by his superior, Detective Superintendent Withers. He looked at Patrick and glanced over at the hurried people in the office behind him. "A new lead?"

"A possible connection." Patrick replied. "It's a loose connection, ropey at best, but it's something. We're going to check for any possible connections between the victims."

Withers nodded in approval. "And CCTV?"

"Officers are collecting it now, and will take it to e-forensics to try and clean it up."

Withers stood in the office and without asking, he closed the door, sealing them both away from the main activity.

"Have you spoken to your brother, Daniel, recently?" he asked.

Patrick stopped short and looked at his superior. Why would he ask about his brother? Why bring him up? Patrick knew he couldn't lie, why would he want to? He hadn't done anything wrong. "I saw him in the smoking shelter after the briefing, then this morning during a family matter."

"And you didn't discuss the murders with him?"

"No I didn't!" Patrick almost snapped. After what he'd been through he wasn't going to fall foul of the media tricks again. "Sir, I understand the Force's concern for the relationship I have with my brother, and I resent the accusation that I would pass him information. He asked questions after the briefing, but I didn't expand on anything that wasn't already stated. He knows where I stand on this matter and he won't pursue me to get information."

"How can you be so sure?" Withers asked.

"He's my brother, and in this family, they will follow my lead."

Withers nodded, but Patrick could see that he wasn't totally convinced.

"What's he done anyway sir?" Patrick asked.

"There was a piece in his paper this morning," Withers said, "it covers the facts as stated in the briefing, but also hypothesises about a lone attacker, who is a stranger to the victims. This wasn't released to the media, so I'm intrigued as to how he got this information."

Patrick looked away from his superior and shook his head. If the accusation of passing information to the press wasn't being made at him, he would've found the situation amusing. "He should've been a police officer." He said to himself.

"Meaning?"

"That's Danny, sir." Patrick explained. "He has a talent of reading between the lines and deducing the truth. When he worked in London, covering Westminster and parliament, he would just say outright that a politician was lying and place the facts of his reasoning at their feet. He ruffled a lot of feathers in Westminster, and a few media giants down there were afraid of the pressure they were getting from the PM and other ministers. So they moved him on." Patrick looked Wither in the eye. "He deduced our murders are the result of a lone stranger attack, not from what I said, but from what I didn't say."

He wasn't sure if Withers was convinced or not. His superior had a perfect poker face, no muscle moved, no twitch or blink of an eye gave any clue to his true thinking. Despite his years and skills of interviewing suspects, Patrick couldn't read Withers at all.

"Just be careful what you say to him will you?" Wither said. "And tell your officers that any information passed to the media via unsanctioned methods will be dealt with at the highest level, and with severe consequences." Withers added as he turned and left Patrick alone in his office.

Patrick sat in his chair and leaned back looking at the ceiling. He could understand the Force's need to ensure the public image of the police was as clean as a virgin's bed sheets, but he resented the implication that he had leaked the details.

He knew the noose of suspicion regarding any leak would always fall around his neck. He had been proved innocent before, but obviously there would be those in the higher echelons who would always suspect him. He had to be careful, and he had to control things as best as he could, without the appearance of creating a cover-up. He made a note of briefing his team before the end of the shift of Withers words, and hoped that the same discipline would be presented by Daniel

*

James walked through the church, and knelt at the steps to the altar. He silently prayed for his lost father and mother, and for all the souls who had departed this world.

They had been instrumental and an important source of encouragement for the path in life he had taken. While his brothers had selected careers that would take them into the city, James had become accustomed to the way of the clergy during his visits to the monastery. As a young teenager he would sit for hours in the chapel and listen to the monks sing. Their soulful melodic choruses would bring a serenity to his heart and mind.

As the years passed he found himself being called to the order and when he was asked at school what career he wanted to follow, he couldn't bring his heart and mind to follow the path of his classmates who wanted to be professional footballers or doctors, actors and millionaires. It was the first time he was faced with the question and as he answered, he felt a wave of emotion fill him. One of contentment, happiness, a self-awareness that told him his choice was the correct path. His teacher didn't say anything, and merely nodded.

That night he told his parents of his plans and they smiled broadly, and almost immediately started to make plans. He had expected his brothers to mock him, and try to convince him to change his mind, but they didn't.

James remembered how he had escaped to the monastery following the incident at the river, and quickly immersed himself in the day to day chores of the monks, praying with them, eating and working with them.

To his surprise, Daniel visited often and together they walked through the grounds, both of them enjoying the tranquillity around them. He knew that Daniel's faith was lacking, and falling away from him, but he still asked questions of his life there, the training and his hopes for the future.

"So you're banned from having sex?" Daniel had asked once with a big smile on his face.

James felt his cheeks flush. "That's the vow you take." He replied, trying to hide his embarrassment.

"Father!" a voice called behind James, pulling him from his memories. He turned around, but couldn't see the source of the voice. He crossed himself and stood up. "Hello?"

"Confession." The voice said.

James looked around him, but couldn't see the person anywhere. As he headed towards the confessional, he saw the curtain move as someone was in there.

James entered the central booth, and pulled the curtain back in the partition of the confessional.

"Bless me Father, for I have sinned." The man said. *"It has been many months since my last confession."*

"Go ahead."

"I have committed a grave atrocity Father, but I have done so at the Lord's command and guidance. I awoke from a sleep of restlessness, seeking a meaning for the pain in the world caused by man. I found myself searching for a meaning of why the world fights against itself, for no other reasons than to advance their own power over their fellow man." The man paused, and James sat silent, listening. *"I found myself walking the streets of the city, seeing the sins of man all around me, the filth, the vile debauchery that society has brought upon itself. Everywhere I looked I saw sinners, and that is when the hand of the Lord took hold of my heart and showed me the way to salvation, not just for myself, but for the world."*

"The Lord shows us the wrongs of other men, but faith will allow the wrongs to be righted." James said quietly.

"They can indeed," the man agreed, *"and the Lord God gave me the strength of will to conduct his vengeance upon the sinners."*

James took a few seconds to reply. "What did he tell you to do?"

The man seemed to think for a moment. *"I have taken lives."* He said. *"I have followed the guidance of the Angels who walk the streets and they have shown me the sinners whose souls need to be returned to heaven to be reborn so that they cannot sin again. I have taken three lives with the sword of Gabriel."*

James allowed the words to sink into his mind, trying to understand the confession. Had this man killed someone? "It is a mortal sin to take another life."

"It was God's will. He guided me and I followed his instructions." The man said. *"I confess my sins and I wish to be absolved."*

James took a breath and thought for a moment. Should he, could he, absolve the sins of a man who has confessed murder? Should he approach the authorities and inform them? During his training at the seminary the students had debated this very action, and the tutor had simply stated that the confessor was seeking forgiveness, and they were not in a position to judge the man for his sins. Only God was worthy of such a task. Man is fallible in his decisions, and if the decision to cleanse him of his sins is wrong, then God would seek that sinner out and cast him from heaven. They should absolve sins, no matter what the confession. "Your actions, while sinful, were allowed by the merciful Lord God." James said. "We are not in a position to question his desires, and as servants of the Lord, we should act as he requires. As penance, recite three Hail Mary's."

The man recited the Act of Contrition and James absolved him of his sins. "Go in Peace."

"Thank you father."

James heard the man move and leave the confessional booth, and he waited a few minutes before himself leaving the booth. He stepped out into the church, expecting to see the man knelt in the pew reciting the prayers, but he wasn't there.

There was no sign of the man anywhere.

James thought about what the man had said. *Could he tell the police about it? Should he violate the sacrament of confession and break his vow to keep Penitent Privilege?* He knew the moral action was to contact the appropriate authorities, but his heart knew that his place in heaven would be cast aside if he was to break his vows, the vows he held so close to his heart.

He had absolved his sins, he thought. That would be enough to stop the man, if he actually did, from committing any further harm to others.

Yes, he thought, the man wouldn't harm anyone else.

CHAPTER 9

Daniel watched the ice cubes swirl around the heavy bottomed glass, slowly melting as the gentle warmth of the scotch whisky devoured it. He liked the small things.

The feel of the glass in his hand.

The noise of the ice cubes landing and tumbling around the bottom of the glass. Drop them from too high and the cubes would crack and splinter, diluting the drink. Let them fall from too low a height, there wouldn't be that *chink* he loved to hear.

He swirled the remaining drops of liqueur around the glass and knocked it back. Before the glass had even hit the bar, he had decided he needed another drink and he caught the bartenders eye.

With a fresh drink in front of him, he took and savoured the first sip. He turned in his seat and looked out across the subdued lighted room of the casino. The gaming floor wasn't busy, with only three roulette tables in use, and there was a bored blackjack dealer, stifling a yawn as she waited for a player to sit at her table and lose their money.

Daniel picked up his drink and headed to the roulette games. He stood and watched the croupier spin the wheel, flick the ball into it and then the punters all sat and watched as the ball span, flicked, clipped and bounced around the wheel until it landed on a number.

Daniel took a seat and pulled a pile of £20 notes from his wallet.

"Changing 200." The croupier called out as she handed back a pile of coloured chips, each worth £10.

To his side, he heard and felt the presence of someone standing next to him. He didn't look up, and placed seven of the chips on the end of the rows on the numbered grid.

"Covering your bases?" Colin Parker asked as he sat down beside him.

"Everyone says they have a system to win on roulette." Daniel replied. "This is mine."

"Does it work?" Colin asked as the ball span around and bounced into the numbered hole.

The croupier reached out and took the chips away, Daniel had lost. "Obviously not." Daniel said.

"You heard then?" Colin Parker asked. Daniel didn't reply and stared at the revolving numbers, waiting for the ball to drop. "We did our best."

Daniel smiled at the comment, but there was no humour behind his eyes. "Our best?" he said. "Our best would've been me keeping my job."

"I wanted to tell you myself." Colin said. "To soften the blow."

"That's very noble of you." Daniel replied, sardonically. "Much better than the letter I found on my desk." he added, pulling a folded piece of paper out of his pocket.

"That's not official yet." Colin said.

Daniel turned to him. "Official or not, I've been fired."

"I'm sorry."

"Yeah, okay. Say it with a bit more sincerity will you." Daniel said as he laid out single chips on different random numbers across the table.

Colin watched as he placed them. "I stood by you Danny. I know the truth about what happened, and I know how good you are. We just couldn't get *them* to see that because all they were worried about was money and the financial implications."

Daniel shook his head. "Don't try and justify it. They wanted me out years ago, and this was their chance."

"There's other things going on." Colin said. "There's a rumour of a corporate take-over, and that story of Marcus Book's son and the drug dealer is going to court."

Daniel nodded in approval as the croupier marked his chip as the winning number and she passed 35 chips to him. "Cash out please." He said to her. He turned back to Colin. "Ironic that I was the one who investigated that story." Daniel said, as he took the collection of chips from the table.

"Perhaps running that story wasn't the best thing either of us should've done. It put us both in the firing line." Colin said, following him to the cash desk.

Daniel scoffed at Colin. "Nobody is above the law." He said as he handed over the chips. "His son broke the law, and his blasé and arrogant attitude made a mockery of the justice system. Marcus Book runs the parent company, not the newspaper. He wanted real life hard hitting stories, where no stone is left unturned, nobody is above the clinical accusatory eye of the public… I think those were his words weren't they? That day he took us over?"

As they headed back towards the bar, Colin remembered the day Marcus Book had risen over their collective horizon and into their lives. *City Times News* had been put up for sale by their previous owner Sir Randolph Sinclair and over a short period of three weeks there was speculation of who would take on the ownership and there was a fierce bidding war.

Finally, the day in July 2009 arrived when Colin had a phone call and he was informed that Marcus Book had bought them.

At the time, he had only heard about Book through hearsay and rumour, and didn't have any particular knowledge of him. It transpired that Marcus Book had made his fortune through the leisure industry, owning nearly 75 health spa and fitness centres across the country. He had then branched out into music, setting up a record label that specialised in discovering new bands and original artists.

As the profile of MBookMusic was starting to gather momentum, Marcus Book took a bold chance and dipped his toes into the murky world of magazines and publishing, purchasing small publishing houses to start his new empire.

When the opportunity for ownership of a newspaper came up, many experts in the media world foretold how Marcus Book would rush to purchase it.

They were right.

As the heavy-set Marcus Theodore Book stood in front of the television cameras on the steps of the newspapers offices, Colin, Daniel, and the majority of the other reporters sat around the televisions in the newsroom to watch their new owner proclaim his vision for the paper.

"Gone are the days of tabloid sensationalism," he proudly pronounced. *"We will deliver hard hitting stories, with a focus on proper journalism. Research and clarification will be the core values I will instil and no stone is left unturned in the search for truth. We live in a social media frenzy, and everyone in public life and those with responsibilities for the well-being of this country should be scrutinised. nobody is above the law, and everyone should be subjected to the clinical accusatory eye of the public."*

Colin remembered the day well, and he recalled how he turned to his staff. "Remember this day," he said, "tough times are coming."

Unfortunately, he didn't know how rough the days would get. As he sat next to his leading reporter, at the bar, he wished he could've helped more to save his friend's job.

"You'll find another job." Colin said.

Daniel laughed, bringing attention to them from other drinkers wishing to forget their own sorrow. "I'm tarnished now. I'm radioactive. Nobody is going to hire me."

There was no denying it, Colin knew he was right. The alleged scandal of passing and receiving information from his brother and back would follow him around for years to come. At best, he thought, Daniel could get a job working at a local newspaper.

He looked at his friend, seeing a beaten defeated man sitting staring at his half-finished drink. Colin knew there was nothing more he could to comfort him. "Danny, I have to go. I'll keep an ear out for any jobs going and let you know."

Daniel didn't respond and stared at the glass before him. *Should he finish it*, he thought. As Colin left him, Daniel took the glass and knocked the drink back in one go and quickly ordered another one.

*

He banged on the door again and leaned against the wall, rubbing his hands on temples. Daniel knew he shouldn't have had the last drink and leaned back, breathing in the cool night air as he heard the door unlock.

The door opened, and Daniel turned to face the woman at the door. She looked at him, with a look of almost distaste. "I thought I told you not to come back."

Daniel stood and faced her, balancing himself against the wall. "H, I've had a crappy day, and I needed to see a friendly face."

"Then you've banged on the wrong door." She replied.

Daniel stepped forward, trying to get in the door. "Can I come in?" he slurred.

But the woman held the door tight. "What are you doing here? We agreed it was over."

Daniel took a step back and looked at her. "You said it was over, I never agreed it was over. It doesn't count H!"

"It does count you drunk fool, and don't call me H!"

"I never ratified it, *Helen*." Daniel said, "A break-up needs to be agreed by both parties for it to be official."

"Well it is Danny." She said sharply. "We had our fun, we both got what we wanted -"

"And then you got tired of me?"

She looked down at him, her patience wearing thin. She wasn't a woman who normally showed emotion, her hardened exterior was a barrier that she fought professionally and personally to keep in place. "Yes." She replied simply. "There was nothing you had that I wanted. I thought there was, maybe you could've helped me progress at work, but you were nothing more than a cheap hack, trying to fuck me for information."

Daniel was trying to form words to speak, but none were coming out of his mouth. He was tired, he was drained, he knew coming to her house was a stupid idea, but he thought he should still try. But as she now talked down to him, her arrogance and strong independence, while admired in the right circumstances, only solidified the iron ice witch persona, he had heard her colleagues describe her as.

When he had first met her, he could sense the emotional hardness within her, but he figured that once they had spent time together, that would thaw and they could progress things further. But he soon learned Helen Kolar wasn't one for thawing. She was strong willed, dominant in the bedroom, but as soon as the deed was done, she was pushing Daniel out of the house.

He turned from the door and headed down the short path towards the road. "You know Helen, I seem to remember you coming round to mine a few months back, asking for a shoulder to cry on after a particular rough day at work. I took you in, no questions asked, and I'm glad to see that kindness being repaid now."

"I wasn't pissed as a skunk!" Helen said.

Daniel turned to her, desperation etched on his face. "I've been fired." He said simply. "I just need – I don't know, I guess I need a friend, someone I can talk to. I know we ended badly, but I'm just asking for someone to give me a break for five minutes."

Helen looked at him, assessing him, as if he was one of the criminals she interviewed at work. He was a pitiful state of a man, she could see it. He was weak, broken, and there was nothing he had that she could utilise for her own needs. But she could see he needed help and reluctantly she stepped to the side to allow him in. "Take a shower first!" she said.

CHAPTER 10

Patrick checked his mobile phone again. Why hadn't she text back, he thought. He had sent Helen Kolar a text the previous night, saying he wanted to see her outside work, but where was her reply? She was usually quick to send a confirmation message, but not hearing from her, meant something was wrong.

"What's wrong with you this morning?" Georgina asked. "You've been checking your phone every minute!"

Patrick looked up at his wife as he sat at the breakfast bar in their kitchen. "I'm expecting a text." He said. "Work."

"Did you hear what I said?" she asked.

Patrick had to admit he hadn't been listening. "Sorry, what did you say?"

Georgina sighed. "I was saying that you need to confirm with your brothers if they'll be coming to Christmas lunch. I know James will be, but you need to speak to Danny. Will he be going to see Louy, or does he want to bring her round here."

"I doubt Samantha would allow that." Patrick said, "You know how hard she kicked Danny around during the divorce to keep custody of Louy, she won't let her come."

"Well ask him anyway." Georgina said, "You may be wrong."

Patrick mumbled that he would and checked his phone again.

Georgina shook her head and turned away from him. Her behaviour didn't go un-noticed by Patrick and he pushed his phone aside. "What!?"

She turned back to him, careful not to raise her voice as both Clarissa and Charlie were in the living room. "It's work again!" she said sharply.

"We have a major investigation going on!"

Georgina shook her head. "It's always something. I know your job, I know you need to be available, but this is the first weekend in months we've had off together as a family, and you're checking your bloody phone again."

"We're going out aren't we?"

"Where?" she asked, partly knowing his response. "Where are we going? Do you even know?"

Patrick looked at her, holding her look, trying to think of their day out. But he couldn't remember. With work, the investigation of the murders, his near infatuation with Helen and their affair, his thoughts were pulled in too many directions for him to keep track of.

"That's what I thought." Georgina said as his silence hung in the air.

"Gee, I'm sorry." He said.

"Do you even know what you're sorry for?" she retorted. "You come home late, or sometimes not at all. You get up and leave before the kids get up. Most of the time you're off work you're on your phone, checking it, texting, or heading back into work. I feel like I'm having a marriage with a ghost."

"I'm here now!"

"Only just! You're checking your phone for messages and you're not listening to me. Obviously work is more important than family."

"That's not true!" Patrick snapped. "Everything I do, I do for this family."

Georgina looked hard at him. "Then do things *with* your family for once."

Neither spoke for a few seconds and the sound of the Saturday morning children's' TV show filtered through to them. Patrick moved first and stepped towards her.

"I know I've been distant recently, but I've got this investigation, the crap from senior management about Danny on top of that too." He said. "Once this enquiry is completed, I'll take some time off, and we can spend it as a family. We have Christmas coming up."

Georgina didn't believe him. "Are you the on-call officer this year?" she asked. She knew he was, he had announced it in November. Once more his silence was all she needed to confirm she was right. "Don't spout statements of you'll be here, when you know damned well there is a very good possibility you won't be."

She stood still as he stepped towards her and she turned from him as he leaned in to give her a consoling hug.

Work would always come before family, she thought as his arms wrapped around her. She gently returned the gesture, but released him quickly.

Patrick released her, knowing deep down there was no feeling behind the action. He had thought about their marriage for a while, where it was going, where it had been. If it would last? He had laid in bed on numerous nights thinking of the best course of action to take. To stay or go. Leave his wife and family, or to stay and continue on the road of wilderness.

He had wondered if he could ever build up the courage of making that decision, but the thought of leaving his children was almost too painful to contemplate. Perhaps, he thought, that was the answer. That was the reason for staying; he could never leave his children. The thought of seeing them on occasional weekends and being brought up by another man, tore at his heart. He saw them sparsely anyway, given his shifts, and to suddenly have more restrictions put on his time with them, was difficult to accept.

But they were old enough to understand that their parents weren't getting along, and to be apart was nothing to do with them, but their parents problems.

Patrick moved away from Georgina and checked his watch. *How long had it been since his text to Helen?* He looked at the bare skin of his wrist, where was his watch? He looked around himself, and checked his pockets. *Where had he left it?*

*

Daniel rolled over onto his side as the sound of the vibrating phone sounded loudly in the bedroom. Wearily he reached out to check it.

He hoped it wasn't work, or his ex-work, he remembered. He hadn't had time to clear his desk the day before, and he had no intention to if he was honest.

Screw them. He had thought as he knocked back the last drink in the casino.

And now that last drink was starting to play hell with his mind. The morning winter sun was low in the sky and was shining in his face.

Wearily he opened his eyes and his mind took a few seconds to try and recognise where he was. It wasn't his flat. But where was he?

He reached for the phone as he sat up and saw the name on the screen.

PATRICK KING

He looked at the phone in confusion as his brother was listed as *PADDY* in his phone. His confusion must've been etched on his face and Helen Kolar entered her bedroom, freshly washed from her shower.

"Never seen a phone before?" she asked.

It took a second before he could form a sentence. "It's my brother." He said finally, "On your phone."

Helen quickly took the phone from him and hung up the call. "I work with him."

Daniel lay back down. He knew they worked together, they had been introduced to each other by Patrick. *But why was he calling her?*

"You can't stay here." She said harshly "You need to go. Now."

"It's Saturday," Daniel said. "Half an hour more."

Helen stood up and rubbed the towel through her hair, exposing her naked body. "Danny, I let you stay. You've over-stayed your welcome already. Do I have to ask again or do I throw you out on your arse?"

Daniel was too tired to argue and slowly pulled the sheets back from his body. "Is there still hot water?"

"Yes," Helen replied, "at your place!"

There was a time, Daniel remembered, when he was considering marrying Helen. But as their relationship had started to dissolve, he had seen the bitterness and hardness of her personality come out.

To some people it would've been an attractive trait to see in her, but after his difficult marriage and subsequent divorce, he didn't want that sort of relationship again, and as he got dressed he knew it was the right decision to leave her. But it was also the wrong decision to have sought her company the night before. He knew he wasn't going to get the attention and compassion he wanted, from her, he never had.

So why did he go there?

He didn't know the answer. Perhaps it was company, sex, the touch of a woman. Maybe he did actually like her and subconsciously sought out her hardened bitterness to make him feel more worthless.

He didn't know why he had gone to her house, and he didn't speak as he pulled his clothes on. As he sat back on the bed to pull his socks on, the sun glinted and reflected off an object on the table. As he pulled his shoes on he looked over at it.

His father's watch.

CHAPTER 11

With Christmas only two weeks away, there were frantic preparations in the church. The manger scene was being constructed, the altar Christmas tree had been purchased and decorated.

Outside, the city centre was adorned with bright lights, snow scenes, outside bars and food stalls, and the now traditional German market.

James was always in two minds about seeing such excess and frivolity. He knew the general public were eager to celebrate Christmas and the New Year in a jovial manner, but there was his more strict religious point of view that the people should be focusing on the real reason for the celebration. The birth of Christ.

Worryingly, he had seen a report on the news that gave a dangerously low percentage of children under 11 who knew the true reason for Christmas. He was eager to try and reverse the all too common thinking that the day was about presents and food, drink and television. He wanted to try and instil a certain amount of charity in the hearts of his congregation.

James had planned for the church to be decorated in a traditional manner, holly, berries, candles and incense. He wanted the vast expanse of the sanctuary to feel warm and welcoming. He wanted the Nativity scene to be as traditional as possible, with the figures all positioned around the crib, at the moment empty until the Christmas Eve mass.

However he was starting to feel like a theatre director in the final days of rehearsals as the helpers he had recruited from the church committee were pestering him for his attention.

"How about these flowers?"

"I think they should be here, Judith says there."

"What about hidden spotlights shining down on the crib?"

The questions bombarded him, and James sat at the end of a pew and rubbed his head.

The pain was muted and dull, but he could feel the familiar throbbing beginning its aching march to the forefront of his head. He needed fresh air, he needed space from the noise.

Leaving the commotion behind, he walked to the big heavy oak doors at the rear of the church and pushed them open.

The cold wind hit his cheeks instantly, but he didn't shy away from the shock. It was what he needed to clear the noise from his mind, the incessant questions and continuous bickering of people who should know better.

Descending the few stone steps to the kerb, he looked back up at the church, seeing the warmth of the glow of lights, diffused by the stain glass windows. He remembered his younger days, his visits to the monastery, and how he had felt the urge to enter and sit quietly in the peace. He had found solace there, and every day he thanked God for the chance to serve Him.

To his side he felt a movement and turned to see a young woman with a child looking at him.

He couldn't speak, he was shocked to see them both. They both looked pale, even in the dying evening light, and he couldn't believe the state of their clothes. Dirty and tattered.

The young boy had a shaggy head of hair, greasy and unkempt. He had wide eyes, almost aghast at seeing him, while his mother looked gaunt and it looked to James as if she had hastily tried to apply make-up in an effort to improve her looks.

The woman spoke. "What's the matter James, aren't you pleased to see your son?"

James still couldn't believe they were there. He took them inside the church and ushered them to a pew near the back. He knew it was a risk to do such a thing, but he hoped the helpers within the church would only think he was talking privately with a woman in need, and not, as it was, him talking to the mother of his secret child.

It would've been more suspicious if he took them into the parochial house, he reasoned, and at least being in the church he could see anyone approaching them, and could change the conversation.

"What are you doing here Anna?" he asked finally, his head hanging low. "We agreed you would never come here, that you would never approach me like this."

Anna sat face on to him, a leg crossed underneath her. James could still see the features of her face that made him so attracted to her all those years before. He recalled the sparkle in her blue eyes, shimmering like the sea, he had once said to her. He had often thought about their first meeting, randomly running into each other as they chased the same taxi, and then sharing the taxi home.

She hadn't been fazed by his profession and role within society, and he soon found her contacting him more and more. They would meet for coffee and he would offer a listening ear as she dealt with personal issues of an abusive partner.

With James' help, Anna had found the courage to leave her partner and on the evening of her brave step out of the relationship, she had insisted on taking him out for a meal.

He accepted and they looked like any other couple sitting in the restaurant, especially as he hadn't dressed in his traditional uniform. The food was good, and the wine was welcomed as they talked about the world, their dreams and hopes. As the evening drew to an end, he found himself kissing her, and then making love to her.

He knew it was wrong and was totally against his vow of abstinence, but the physical pleasure that flowed through him was too great to simply end and forget. But when Anna announced her pregnancy, James had faced one of the biggest decisions of his life.

He had confided in Daniel what had happened, and he had listened to James as his plight was explained. Daniel had offered words of advice, telling him that he should follow his heart, and if that route told him to continue being a priest, then he should follow it.

James had thought about the repercussions from the Church should they ever find out about the boy, Tom. He recalled what Daniel had said:

"I don't think you're the first priest in the Catholic church to father a child, and I doubt there was never a pope throughout history who had done the same."

James didn't appreciate the flippancy of the remark, the insinuation. But he understood the meaning and he knew within him that Daniel was right. But those occasions occurred in different times in history when the power of the church was unyielding and the faith of the congregation stronger, and an unwanted pregnancy could be blamed on the work of the Devil, rather than the urges of man.

Daniel looked around the church, at the altar, the crucifix, the stained glass windows, and the mural on the wall depicting a fight between an angel and a demon. "Why are you here?" he asked, not looking away from the image.

"We need help." Anna said softly.

"There are other churches, other places you could go to." James replied turning to her, trying not to get drawn to her eyes, or her too low cut shirt, showing the rounded edge of her breasts.

Anna shook her head. "I don't need *that* help, Jimmy, I need money."

"I send money." He said, making a mental calculation of the money he had sent her from a secret account set up by Daniel for him. "I send more than I should."

Her eyes were starting to fill with tears. "I know, I know you do, and I'm thankful for every penny. Tom is thankful. But -"

"You need more." James interrupted.

It had been 6 years since Tom had been born and he had tried to see his son at least once a year, although Tom was never told of their relationship. James had also paid more than he should've to help them both survive, and he had vowed and told Anna he wouldn't pay more than they had already agreed. "How much more?" he found himself asking.

Anna looked up to him and placed a hand on his arm. "Two thousand."

James had to control himself from shouting at her, and he shrugged her arm away. "That's ridiculous. I don't have that money."

"But you can get it!" Anna said, grabbing his arm. "You can get it!"

He looked at her, seeing her blue eyes harden for a second. "Where? Where can I get it?" he said harshly.

Anna looked around herself and nodded at the altar, as if to say *"From here."*

James shook his head. "I'm not stealing from the Church."

"You're not stealing. It'll be helping the needy." Anna said, her hands gripping him tightly. "You once said, when I first found out about being pregnant, that you would do anything to help me."

"That was before I decided to stay with the church."

"But you said it!" Anna said, "You're heart told you to say it, because that is the type of person you are. You help people. Look at your son Jimmy. He needs clothes, he needs a meal. I can't give that to him."

"What about the money I send? Where's that gone?"

Anna released her grip and sank back into the pew. "Rent, heating, bills, the usual things."

"I thought you had a job?"

Anna let out a laugh that echoed around the church, bringing attention to them from those by the near constructed nativity scene. "I got fired."

"And what do you think will happen to me if it was discovered I was stealing from the church?" James asked.

"Bigger things have been covered up within the Church Jimmy!"

James shook his head in disgust, remembering the similar comment from Daniel when he learned of Anna's pregnancy. With all the great work the church had done over the years, with the teachings, the moral guidance and the feasts of Easter and Christmas that the majority of the country, including atheists enjoy celebrating, he still found it frustrating that the general public still reverted back to the controversies within the church.

He wanted to tell her to leave, to never contact him again, and he wanted to cut off the funds he wilfully paid her. But he knew that she would threaten to approach a newspaper and expose their relationship and child to the world. It would mean the end of his career, he would be defrocked and excommunicated from the church. He would be humiliated and wouldn't be able to get another job, not that there was another job he wanted.

He had dedicated his life to the teachings of the Church, and knew he wasn't in a position at the moment to throw it all away. *But could he do that?* He asked himself. *Could he really give up all the years of hard work, the dedication, the spiritual searching of doubt he had endured?*

His parents had supported him through-out his initial decision, through his studies and ordination, and to leave it all behind, for this woman, a woman he wasn't sure he even loved? No, he thought, he could never leave the Church.

James had always strived to help, no matter who was in need. He wasn't the type of person to turn his back on people when they needed help, and he certainly never wanted to be a father who would watch his son suffer, even if he wasn't a particular traditional father-figure.

He watched as the church helpers allowed Tom to help decorate the nativity scene at the front of the church. He saw the smile on the boy's face as he placed the flowers at the direction of the women. James watched as Tom asked questions, pointing to the figures of Mary and Joseph, and then to the empty crib.

He was learning about the true meaning of Christmas, James thought, and he fought hard to keep his emotion and pride within him.

He turned back to Anna. "I'll see what I can do."

Anna thanked him and quickly moved in and kissed him on the cheek. As she moved close, he caught the wisps of her perfume that brought back so many memories of their time together.

As he sat transfixed in his memories, he heard Anna call Tom and they left him alone, thinking of the past. It took a few moments for the memories to dissipate and he slowly headed back towards the front of the church. He didn't know how he could actually take money from the church accounts without being discovered, but he knew he must try.

As he neared the front, the nattering voices of the helpers began to gnaw at his brain once more and he made an excuse that he wasn't feeling too well and headed out of the church.

<u>PART THREE</u>

GREED

CHAPTER 12

It had been another long day for Clive Lancashire, and as the automatic gates opened to allow his driver to take him the final few yards to his front door, he was relieved to be home once more.

At 58 years old, he was starting to feel the miles of traveling to New York and back within a week. He had promised his wife Jessica that it would be his last overseas trip, or at least the last one without her, he thought. The meetings in New York were productive, and with new contracts ready to be signed, Clive was sure his company would make a decent percentage profit the following year.

The loose stones of his drive-way crunched underneath the weight of the car, and stepping out into the cold night air, he looked up at the pillared porch decorated in small Christmas lights.

His driver put his bags down on the steps. "Is that all sir?"

"Yes, thank you. I'll take them in, have a good evening."

"You too sir."

Clive, despite his wealth and success in the business world, was still uncomfortable with being *sir*, and the privilege of having a personal driver was an extravagance he enjoyed after long journeys, but not necessarily all the time. But if the company was willing to pay for the privilege, so be it, he thought.

With only a few more steps to go to the warmth of home, he picked up his bags and entered his grand house.

Inside he smelt the familiar aroma of the open fire, mingled with the scented candles and there, in front of him a large pine Christmas tree, reaching up into the double height space of the stair well that encircled the tree.

He was home, and he smiled.

Dropping his bags by the stairs he walked into the living room and saw next to the fire, lying lazily in the warmth of the flames, his two dogs. They were asleep and breathing heavily, and he smiled to himself as he recalled the days when he would be greeted with the sounds of three children running at him and knocking him to the floor. Despite his tiredness at returning from another long trip, he would always be invigorated by the greeting he got from them.

It was just the passage of time, he thought, as he headed to the kitchen to find his wife.

But she wasn't there.

In the oven, he saw the roast dinner cooking slowly, bubbling away in its own juices, and he suddenly realised it was the small things he missed when he was away, such as a home cooked meal.

"Jess?" he called, but there was no answer.

He climbed the stairs and headed towards their bedroom. He heard the soft music playing from their room and slowly he opened the door. He could see the mirror on the wardrobe door, and in the reflection, the edge of the bed where there was a black, lacy negligee laid out on the bed.

Welcome home! He thought.

Both he and his wife may have been in their 50's, but they still enjoyed a sex life that was better than most people half their age.

Sex and a roast dinner. If she throws in a beer too, he thought, *she may get a diamond for Christmas.*

He entered the bedroom and saw the negligee on the bed and the ran his fingers across it, and with his eye catching the sight of the trail of rose petals he took his jacket off and followed them to the en-suite bathroom.

The bathroom was full of steam from the shower, and he heard the water pouring down. He could feel the excitement within him grow and he pulled his shirt and tie off, tossing them to the side. Within seconds, his shoes, socks, and trousers were off too, and, as he stood at the shower curtain, he took his boxer shorts off, happy seeing that he was ready for some much needed sexual attention.

He pulled back the curtain and stared as he saw Jessica, his wife, lying crumpled down in the cubicle, blood covered and soaking wet. She was naked, pale, all life seeping out of her as it ran down the drain.

Clive shouted out and reached down to her, calling her name and checking her. Her blood covered his hands and he told her to keep breathing. He saw her eyes move and he gave a weak smile.

"Stay with me Jess," he cried, "Oh god, please stay with me!"

Clive scrambled away from the shower and ran into the bedroom reaching for the phone and dialling 999.

"Ambulance!" he shouted down the phone. "Quick, my wife's been attacked, she's in the shower bleeding!"

He tried to answer the questions the operator was asking, but his mind was a chaotic mess of thoughts. "Just get here now!" he shouted down the phone once he gave the address.

With the phone in his hand he headed back into the bathroom and stopped short as he saw a man in a black hood standing before him.

"Who're you? WHAT DO YOU WANT!?" Clive shouted.

The man took a step forward, and Clive took a moment to recognise the face beneath the hood.

"YOU??" he said and gasped as the attacker pushed a knife into Clive's body.

The man pulled the knife out and stabbed him again, pushing the blade deeper into his body. Clive dropped the phone and shouted out for help as he dropped to the floor reaching out to touch his wife once more before they were reunited in the afterlife.

Beside him, the emergency operator was calling out for Clive, asking him what was happening, but there was no reply. The hooded man picked up the phone and listened to the near frantic calls from the operator and calmly, he disconnected the call.

Wiping the blade of the knife on the white towels, the man stepped over the body of Clive and into the bedroom. He headed to the doorway and as he left, he dropped a sheet of paper: *GREED*.

CHAPTER 13

Daniel looked at the watch in his hand and turned it over. The inscription on the back was still legible and he read it again.

To my husband, on our anniversary xx

It was a present from his mother to his father, and it had been passed down from their father to Patrick. Passed to the eldest, and favourite son, the son who could do no wrong.

Daniel shook his head at the thought. *Could do no wrong?* He was having an affair, risking everything from his family to his career. *Would their father be so accepting of Patrick's behaviour if he knew about that now?*

He didn't know what to do.

Since leaving Helen Kolar's house he had turned the information over in his mind. The phone call from his brother and the manner in which Helen had simply dismissed it bothered him.

It was as if she was comfortable enough to dismiss his call with no fear of the consequences, despite him being her boss. That was either brave of her, and demonstrated once more her brash personality, or there was something else.

The only way he could describe it to himself was if she was dismissing it because she had had a lot of contact with him, or she was trying to hide their contact from Daniel.

He knew that on its own, there wasn't much information to form a proper reasonable argument for the behaviour, but with the discovery of the watch, that changed the meaning of everything. On its own, a missed phone call meant nothing, but the watch was more significant.

Daniel tried to work out how the watch had been left there. *Had he dropped it at work; took it off and forgotten to pick it up? Had he took it off when the team had gone out for drinks and Helen picked it up?*

Or had he taken it off when he had been in her house?

All were possible, but the underlying problem Daniel had was that it was in the bedroom.

If Helen had picked the watch up in innocent circumstances, why would it be in the bedroom? Why wasn't it in the living room?

He couldn't work out any scenario that fitted the facts, other than one; and Daniel didn't like it.

He knew he had to say something, he had to do something to stop his brother from destroying his home life, destroying his family, and destroying his career.

After an hour of sitting outside Patrick's house, Daniel finally made a decision and headed to the front door, ready to confront his brother.

He stood on the doorstep waiting for the door to be answered. As the seconds passed, he had no idea what he would say, what the first words would be. Should he just come out and tell him what he thought? Should he lay down the evidence there and then?

As he heard the footsteps approach the door he prepared himself for the confrontation.

Georgina opened the door and Daniel was momentarily taken aback. "Hi." He said finally.

Georgina looked surprised too. "I thought you were Patrick."

"Surely he would have a key?"

Georgina smiled at him, and Daniel thought as if it was a relief smile, one given as tension was released. "He went out earlier, left his keys."

Daniel looked back over his shoulder at the car on the driveway. "His car's here."

"He took mine." She said. "Do you want to come in?"

Daniel paused for a moment, and he thought he could hear a crack of emotion in her voice. "You okay?"

She nodded and headed back into the house, allowing Daniel to follow her in.

The coffee tasted good. Proper filter coffee that stimulated the senses and memories similar to summer mornings and freshly cut grass.

Taking a sip, Daniel gave a smile to Georgina. "I should buy some of this decent stuff. I've only got the cheap crap."

Georgina was sitting opposite him at the breakfast bar and she ran her hands through her auburn hair. In the light of the kitchen, Daniel could see her reddened eyes and damp cheeks as if she had been crying. He didn't want to upset her any more than she already clearly was. He wanted to know what had happened, but he didn't know how. Seeing her like that, upset, emotional, he suddenly felt the urge to reach out and hold her.

"You've changed your hair." He said finally.

Georgina gave a short laugh. "At least someone noticed."

"Bit hard not to notice, it really suits you."

She smiled at him, and Daniel could see there was a genuine warmth there at the compliment.

"So where is he?" Daniel asked.

She took a deep breath and let it out as she spoke. "Oh – I don't know. Work I think. We were meant to have the weekend together. With his stupid shift patterns we don't get much time together as a family, but instead of going to the science centre today, he got a phone call to go into work. I asked him not to, but, well you know your brother."

Daniel took a sip of his drink, giving himself a chance to think. *Was there really an issue at work that needed his attention, or was there a woman needing his attention?* Perhaps he had been mistaken and the phone call to Helen was to get her into work too. *But what about the watch?* His mind always returned to the watch and it being there at Helen's house. There was no other possible way for it to get there than if left by Patrick.

Daniel looked at his sister-in-law and saw her shoulders sagging, her head low, she looked tired as if fighting a long hard battle. "Are you guys okay?"

Georgina shrugged, trying to keep the tears from her eyes. "I don't know. I keep trying to talk to him about things, but he brushes me off or says not to worry."

"His work is stressful, and with what's going on -"

"He's had busy times before," she interrupted. "This is, I don't know, this is different."

A silence fell between them again and they looked at each other. As he looked into her eyes, he recalled the times they spent together as kids. He remembered how they would be inseparable, meeting before school, sitting in class together, eating lunch together, and walking home together. After school, weekends and in the holidays, they would spend near enough every waking moment together.

But then they were teenagers and Daniel started to see her in a different light, especially as her young womanly form took shape. Their friendship continued to grow and during the summer holidays, aged 15, they stole their first kiss from each other.

They had been sitting on the edge of the river bank, sitting comfortably in the silence between them, and then their hands brushed against each other. They were both nervous and as their hands and fingers closed around each others, they leaned in and kissed.

He could still remember the feeling of her lips on his, still feel the sensation as they kissed, and he knew that was the moment he fell in love with her.

"What are you thinking about?" Georgina asked, bringing his attention back to the kitchen.

"Silly memories," he said, "that day the two of us were by the river."

She laughed and covered her mouth, embarrassed. "Oh god, yes! I was so nervous."

"Me too."

She smiled at him. "Our first kiss."

"Our only kiss." Daniel said, mournfully. "Wished there could've been more."

As soon as he had spoken, he regretted it. Daniel wasn't a person to publicly expose and show his emotions, and he internally cursed himself for saying it.

He didn't know what made him say it, but he could sense it was time to leave. "I should go." He said, picking up his coat and leaving the kitchen before Georgina could say anything.

At the front door, he pulled his coat on and adjusted the collar as Georgina opened the door for him. He was about to leave when she closed it. "I wish there had been more kisses too Danny." She said.

Daniel looked at her and before he could say anything, her lips were on his, her hands around his neck and she pushed him back against the door.

Daniel couldn't believe what was happening, but he found his hands were pulling her closer to him, running up her back, and finding a route underneath her shirt, feeling her soft skin.

He didn't want the moment to end.

With every passing second, their kissing was frantic, more eager, as if years of pent up frustration were about to be unleashed. Daniel's coat had been pulled off and Georgina was pulling his shirt out of his trousers as they made their way to the living room.

They fell on the sofa, Daniel above her, kissing her lips and neck. His hands moved over her body and he gentle squeezed her breasts as his mind took in every feeling of her.

They momentarily stopped and looked at each other, there was no embarrassment or guilt, it felt normal, and Georgina pulled him down onto her and kissed him again.

"You're vibrating." She said, giggling.

"You have that effect on me." Daniel said, kissing her neck.

"No," she replied moving back, "I mean you're phone is vibrating."

Daniel laughed and pulled out his phone. "I was just happy to see you."

As he answered the phone, Georgina sat close to him, gently running her fingers down his back. She knew it was wrong what she had done, but she hadn't had any physical attention for months, and the urges were too strong to resist. She suddenly wanted this man, no matter what relation he was to her.

"When did it start?" Daniel asked into the phone, seriousness back in his voice. "Okay, try and keep him calm, I'll be there as soon as I can."

He hung up the phone and turned to her. "I have to go."

"What's happened?"

He stood up and buttoned his shirt. "That was Fr. William at the church. It's Jimmy, he's having an episode."

Georgina stood too. "Oh god. I thought he had recovered."

"Something must've triggered it. I'm sorry."

"What for?"

Daniel pulled his coat on. "For what happened now." To his surprise Georgina stepped forward and kissed him on the lips again.

"I'm not." She said. "You go and help your brother, we can pick this up later."

Daniel smiled at her and kissed her again, hugging her and allowing himself to be with her for a moment. Releasing her, he headed to the door and opened it.

"Text me later?" she asked.

He turned back to her and kissed her again on the cheek. "I will."

CHAPTER 14

The front door was opened to the parochial house before Daniel had reached it, and Fr. Martin directed him upstairs. "Fr. William is up there."

Daniel took two stairs at a time and was soon outside the bedroom door where a pensive William was pacing. Daniel had met both William and Martin on a number of occasions, when he had visited James. Despite his own rejection of the Catholic teachings, he still admired his brother's dedication and obedience of the religion. When he was younger he found himself asking questions that the church couldn't answer, and when he was directed to find the answers in the bible he was met with what he thought were riddles and convoluted passages that could be interpreted a thousand different ways. He soon became disillusioned with the archaic teachings, and when James announced his intentions of joining the priesthood, Daniel had to reign back his condemnation of the church and decided to support his brother.

"Where is he?" he asked.

William nodded at the bedroom door. "He's in there. He came back around two hours ago, and I could see he wasn't himself. He talked differently, calling himself *Dante*, and then came up here."

"We heard banging and loud noises," Martin added, "and it was if he was talking to someone in there."

"But there's nobody in there?" Daniel asked.

The two priests shook their heads. "No."

"What about contacting the Bishop?" Martin asked.

Daniel turned to him, "Why?"

"To help us pray." Martin replied. "It's as though our brother is possessed."

"He's not possessed." Daniel said. "He has some mental health problems that the Bishop is well aware of. To bring him down here would be a waste of his time. I can sort this."

"What sort of mental health issues?" William asked.

Daniel took his jacket off. Despite their simple living, the priests enjoyed the warmth of a cosy house. "Nothing serious, but he needs regular medication. I'm guessing he didn't take it for whatever reason."

Without waiting for another question, he entered the bedroom.

Closing the door behind him, Daniel stepped into the room. A single lamp illuminated the bed in the corner of the room. Sparsely decorated, the only items were a wardrobe, bed, table and chair, and on the wall a crucifix and a picture of the current Pontiff.

In the dim light Daniel could see the shape of James lying on the bed, and as he stepped closer, he could hear the calm, repetitive breathing of his brother. He pulled a chair over to the side of the bed and sat down.

James was sweating, his matted damp hair stuck to the pillows and his scalp. His chest was rising and falling quickly and his body jerked as if a shock had been sent through his body. It wasn't the first time Daniel had seen his brother in such a state, but whenever he did, he couldn't help but feel compassion and love to try and help him. James had faced too many demons in his life and Daniel had vowed to help him through it all.

He reached out and touched his brother. "James?" he whispered. "It's Dan."

James stirred and rolled over, squinting in the low light as he saw his brother. His red damp, swollen eyes almost glowing. "What are you doing here?"

Daniel quickly explained that William and Martin were concerned about him and had called him over.

"I'm fine," James said wearily . "I've had my drugs. I'm fine." He turned back towards the wall and Daniel sat back. He looked around and saw the empty medication packets on the floor.

"What happened?" Daniel asked.

"It doesn't matter." James replied, muffled as he buried his face in the quilt.

"It does," Daniel said, "come on, tell me. I can help."

James rolled back over and faced his brother. Tears were rolling down James's cheeks and the emotion of the moment caught hold of him. "I almost betrayed the Church." He said. "I was touched by evil and contemplated stealing from the Church."

Daniel grabbed his brother's hand and held it tight, himself trying to hold back the tears as he watched his brother battle with his emotions. "Why would you do that?"

"Anna." James said. "Anna turned up wanting more money."

"She came back here? You spoke to her?"

James nodded. "Yes. She had Tom with her, and she said she needed more money. I told her I didn't have it, but she insisted and suggested I take money from the Church."

"Did you?"

He shook his head. "By the grace of God I didn't. But I couldn't get the thought of Tom suffering out of my head. I couldn't stay here."

"So you went out?"

"And I missed my medication time."

Daniel nodded. He understood.

The medication James was on needed strict time control to keep the dosage within his system at an optimum level. To miss the timing would have an adverse effect on him.

"You can't give her any more money." Daniel said.

"I know. But I don't know what else to do."

Daniel sat back for a moment and thought. He admired that his brother was still willing to help Anna with money, but there was a limit to what he could do for her.

She couldn't keep demanding money off James when she felt like it, there was an agreement in place, and she was breaking the rules set out.

"Where is she?" he asked.

"Why?" James asked.

"I'll go and see her." Daniel said.

James sat up and wiped his face. "No Dan, no. You'll make things worse."

"She can't keep doing this."

"But I need to help her, I need to help my son!"

Daniel shook his head. "I love your dedication brother, but you have to see that this isn't the way to continue."

"But -"

"What?" Daniel interrupted. " But what?"

"I won't see Tom." James said.

"And how often do you see him now?" Daniel said. "You need to realise you will never have the same father – son relationship with him. You made a choice, a difficult choice, but also the right choice. You're doing what you can with the limited freedom you have. She can't just show up, asking for money, then disappear for months at a time. How much did she ask for? How much money?"

"Two thousand."

Daniel looked at him, wide eyed. "Okay, we definitely need to do something. I'll need to tell Patrick though."

A look of confusion crossed James' face. "Tell him what?"

"About Anna and Tom."

"He doesn't know?"

Daniel shook his head. "No. You asked me not to tell him and I didn't."

"But that was 6 years ago?!"

"And I've stayed quiet for 6 years." Daniel replied. "This is your business, and I'll only tell people if I have your blessing."

James looked at is brother, and patted his hand, the emotion straining on his voice. "People always misjudged you Danny. You're more loyal than any other man I know."

Daniel shrugged off the compliment with a smile. "Yeah I know – God can thank me if I get to heaven!"

CHAPTER 15

He banged on the door again and waited for a reply, it was the third time, and Daniel wasn't going to leave until she had answered. He had already tried Patrick's office number, but there was no reply, and he wasn't picking up his mobile phone. Hoping he wasn't correct, he had headed over to Helen Kolar's house and when he saw Georgina's car parked outside, his heart sank. "I hate being right.", he said to himself just as he went to bang on the door again. Helen answered it.

"Oh, it's you." She said sharply. "You can't come in."

Daniel hated the manner in which she spoke to him and he turned to her. "I'm not here for you."

"Then why are you here?"

Daniel nodded towards the bedroom upstairs. "Tell my brother to get dressed and meet me in my car."

Helen was silent for second as he turned away from her and headed back to his car. "He's not here." She said, but her voice cracked as she tried to regain her composure.

How did he know Patrick was there? How did he find out?

Daniel turned back to her at the bottom of the path. "Tell him to put his dick away and get down here." He said as he opened the car door and climbed in.

Helen didn't have time to speak again and she closed the door and headed up to Patrick, lying naked on her bed.

It took another 15 minutes before Patrick skulked out of the house, like a petulant teenager who had been caught smoking.

Daniel could see the hypocrisy of him berating his brother for being unfaithful, he had after all kissed his sister-in-law. But that was different, he told himself. Daniel wasn't married and he wasn't cheating on anyone. And Georgina? She was only looking for affection and attention, as Patrick had neglected her for so long.

He reasoned that if Patrick hadn't started the relationship with Helen Kolar, then he and Georgina wouldn't have kissed and stirred up long forgotten emotions within him.

Patrick got into the car and no sooner had the door closed than Daniel was driving away.

The silence in the car was tense. Daniel had so much to say, he didn't know where to begin. He knew his brother well enough that should he start with any accusations, Patrick would either dismiss them out of hand or go on the attack, dragging up Daniel's own errors in life, including his gambling habit.

He wanted Patrick to feel his nerves strain as the silence continued. He wanted to make Patrick suffer for risking his marriage and the happiness of Georgina on his actions and he continued to drive in silence.

Patrick was nervous, he had been caught out, literally with his pants down. He didn't know how Daniel had found him, but he wanted to know. He needed to know.

Had he told Georgina? Was his marriage now over?

He knew he should speak first. As the elder brother, he still had some sway over Daniel. He still saw himself as the head of the family since their father had died. His decisions, Patrick believed, should always be considered the most appropriate and best course of action. It was how their father headed the family, and it was how he wanted it to be. Daniel could be manipulated, he thought.

They had had many arguments over the years, and he knew Daniel would want to get all of the accusations out of the way as soon as possible, and then when he had extinguished all of his arguments, Patrick would calmly plough through them, picking them apart and dissecting them for flaws and contradictions. All he had to do was wait.

But Daniel didn't say a word. He continued to drive and was focused on the road ahead. Patrick had to say something.

"Where are we going?"

Daniel didn't look at him as he answered. He couldn't, he was so angry, but finally he spoke. "Seven years ago, James got a woman pregnant. He had completed his training and had just been ordained."

"He did what? What the hell –" Patrick said, but Daniel continued talking, ignoring his outburst.

"Since then he's been paying maintenance to the woman and boy, Anna and Tom, using an account I set up in my name on his behalf. This afternoon Anna approached James and demanded more money off him. He was stressed, pissed off and didn't take his meds and he had an episode. He had calmed down when I got there."

"How is he?"

Daniel focused on the road as he answered. "He's coping. He has months of being fine and then something could kick it off. Usually stress, like this woman turning up.."

"Does the church know?"

"The archbishop knows about his meds situation, but not about Anna." Daniel said. "I've sat down with the archbishop and we've discussed what we can do to help him with his meds."

Patrick sat back in the seat. "Why wasn't I told about this?"

Daniel shot him a look. "You don't have to know everything. James didn't want to tell you, so I kept my word."

"Why didn't he tell me?"

"You'll have to ask him," Daniel said.

A silence fell on them again and the streets passed them by. "So where are we going?" Patrick asked.

"To speak to this Anna woman."

Patrick couldn't believe it. *James had fathered a child? Why wasn't he told?*

"How could he be so bloody stupid?" Patrick said. "He could ruin his life!"

Suddenly Daniel hit the brakes of the car hard and pulled them to a stop with the screeching of tires. He turned to Patrick. "Don't you dare!" he snapped. "Don't you dare sit there and lecture me or him about the virtues of honesty and integrity! How dare you even think you can take a righteous path at the moment."

"You don't know shit about what's going on with me!" Patrick said.

"Paddy!" Daniel said, holding up his hand to stop him talking. "I've got a hundred things going on at the moment and I can only deal with 24 of them at one time. You and your over sexed loins are number 51. So I'll get to you as and when I'm ready."

As fast as the car had stopped, Daniel hit the accelerator and he sped away, not caring that he was speeding with a police officer in his car.

The remainder of the journey was in silence as the two brothers watched the road. Daniel had formulated a plan for their impromptu meeting with Anna, and as he turned into the road and parked the car he finally spoke to Patrick about it.

"We're going in to talk to her." He said. "She needs to stop harassing James."

"And how do you propose to do that?" Patrick asked.

Daniel looked at him. "For however long this takes, you're not a police officer. You're a brother helping his family."

Daniel climbed out of the car quickly followed by Patrick. "What do you mean by that?" Patrick asked.

Daniel turned to him. "I've met this woman before, and I know what she's like. She is one of those people who will demand something off anyone because you have it, and she doesn't. She thinks she has a goddamn right to everything because of her self-imposed importance." *Like you,* he wanted to say, but refrained himself.

They continued down the street and Daniel found the house and knocked on the door.

"We shouldn't do this." Patrick said.

Daniel banged hard on the door again. "Yes," he said casting a quick look at him, "yes we should."

The door was answered by a young man, piercings haphazardly stabbing his face and lip. A tattoo reached up from under his vest and onto his neck. "Yeah?"

"We're here to see Anna." Daniel said.

"She's not in."

Daniel pushed the door back as the pin cushion man started to close it. "You won't mind if we post a note under her door then will you?"

Without waiting for a reply, Daniel pushed past the man and headed upstairs towards the next flat. Patrick was close behind him and they found Flat 2. Daniel knocked the door and was slightly taken aback as the door was opened.

Anna was as he remembered her. Short, with longish brown hair. Her makeup was excessively applied and in her fingers was a lit cigarette. "Who're you?" she asked.

"We've met before." Daniel said. "James King's brothers."

Anna seemed to give a sly smile. "You have my money?"

"No." Daniel said simply. "Can we come in?" he added as he pushed past her.

Anna tried to stop him, but instead decided to let him enter. "Doesn't look like I can stop you."

Daniel looked around the flat. A small kitchenette was in the corner of the living room, that doubled for a bedroom. There was a curtained off area that he guessed was the bathroom. All over the floor were dirty plates and clothes. Broken toys were scattered everywhere and in the bed asleep was Tom. Against the wall was a TV showing whatever the newest reality TV program sensation was on that week, Daniel hadn't a clue. He scanned all the items and then faced Anna.

"You're going to stop contact with James, now" he said. "You're not going to get the two grand off him, so don't bother to ask."

Anna gave a smile. "Well I think that's an issue between me and Jimmy." She nodded at Tom. "That's his son, it's his duty to look after him."

Daniel didn't take his eyes off her. "And he will do what's right. But he won't be made a fool of and he won't be blackmailed."

"Blackmail?" Anna repeated with a snort. "I'm trying to provide a future for my son, and he needs to pay up."

"So you can piss it away?"

"How dare -"

Daniel held up a hand and cut her short. "Please. Stop. You have a 45 inch plasma TV there, £150 designer boots on your feet, a gold – what is it? 24 carat necklace on.

There's a game console and a dozen games, a few expensive bottles of whisky and vodka on the side and on the coffee table are car keys. Which, if I can make a bold guess, will be for the '59 plate vehicle outside."

Patrick looked around and noted each of the items Daniel had mentioned. They had been in there less than a minute and his brother had made a mental note of everything in the blink of an eye. He could only admire his brother's perception skills

Daniel paused as he allowed his observations to be understood. "I don't know what scam you have going on," he continued, "but I bet you don't need his money, so – you won't get any."

"You have no right -" Anna started to say.

"And you sweetheart have no right to play James for a fool." Daniel interrupted. "You know, we've met before. When all of this started I came to see you, do you remember?"

Anna looked at him, trying to place him. He looked familiar, but maybe that was because of his shared genes with James. She couldn't remember if she was honest, she had had a few too many drink and drug binges to allow her to remember clearly.

"Yeah," Daniel continued. "I came to your flat, you lived somewhere else at the time. I wanted to speak to you about what had happened and when I arrived I found you shacked up with some other man. A big brute, King Kong sort of half ape half man thing. Looked like he was wearing a jumper he was that hairy. Anyway, he told me in no uncertain terms to piss off, which is what I did. But on the way out I spoke to one of your house mates and they said that you and Kong had been together for about 2 years already and that you were pregnant with his child."

Anna suddenly stopped moving and looked at him. Patrick too stood silently as Daniel took a step forward. His police training was starting to kick in, he was watching the scene unfold and he was getting ready to act should the need call for it. He was listening to his brother talk, as eloquently as his writing, but he couldn't see the end point.

"What I'm saying," Daniel said calmly, "is that I don't think for one moment that Tom is James' son. I don't doubt you slept with my brother, but I bet you did so you could say you were knocked up and then ask him for money. My brother is naïve when it comes to the ways of the world. He lives in it, preaches about it, but can never see the true face of it. He felt so strongly to help, he would've believed anything you told him."

Anna was silent as Daniel continued to talk.

"So, here's what's going to happen. You're going to take this month's money, but then that's it, nothing more. I'm going to shut the account down and you'll not get another penny. Feel free to go and shout at the newspapers and cameras saying a priest got you pregnant. The Catholic Church has one of the best public relations departments in the world, I think they could take you on."

He took a step closer to her, intimidating her, and she moved away from him. "But one of the first thing's they'll ask for is a DNA test." He said. "And that darling, is where your plan will come unstuck." He looked around them at the flat. "And should a phone call be made to the appropriate department at social services, I think it's fair to say this isn't the ideal place to house a child."

"Are you threatening me?" Anna asked, fear and realisation that she had been caught out etched on her face.

Daniel looked at her hard. "Promising you darling." He headed to the door and opened it, turning back to her. "Game's over." He said, and left the flat with Patrick following.

CHAPTER 16

Patrick watched the dark city streets pass them by as Daniel drove. He was appalled at the manner in which his brother had handled Anna, and he was disgusted with himself for letting it happen.

Why had he even taken Patrick along?

Was it to prove that he knew about his affair with Helen?

Patrick still felt numb at the thought that his infidelity had been found out, and he still wanted to know how. But he knew that to ask questions, would weaken his position on what he still thought was, the higher moral ground. How dare his brother question his actions, he thought.

He would admit that his relationship with Georgina over the past year or so had become stale, and they weren't as close as they once were. He had faced rejection from her for his advances for sex for many years, and had simply accepted the state of their sex life. But then he met Helen

Kolar and had found his desire to resurge. He was doing it for his own mental well-being, and whatever Georgina was doing for hers, was her own business.

This was how Patrick would deal with his problems.

"I should've stopped you." He said to Daniel. "That was no way to deal with her."

"It's done." He replied. "She'll back off and leave James alone, allowing him to carry on in peace."

"There's no way of knowing that for sure." Patrick said.

Daniel ignored him. He knew his brother was right, there was no way of knowing if she would back off. His threat to her was an empty threat. He wasn't the type of man to bring more suffering to a single mother and her son. But he had to give the impression he would do it. That was why he was so hard with her.

"And what are you going to tell Jimmy?" Patrick asked.

Daniel paused for a moment. He hadn't thought that far ahead. He knew if he was to tell James the truth in that he had confronted her and blackmailed her, he would not take it well, and with James' current relapse in his mental well-being, he could suffer another set-back. "I'll think of something." He said simply.

"He was a fool to get into something like this." Patrick said absently.

Daniel shook his head, unable to accept the hypocrisy. "I find it difficult to listen to your righteous condemnation of James, considering the shit you're about to put your family through."

"And there it is!" Patrick retorted harshly. "Come on, say what you want to say."

Daniel shot him a glance, "Why? So you can twist my words to make you sound justified in what you're doing?"

"No," Patrick snapped. "I want to hear the words of enlightenment that has steered you so well through these years. Forgetting your own chequered past and how many was it? Three affairs you had?"

Daniel stayed quiet for a moment. He knew his brother was trying to antagonise him, to make him lose his focus and therefore his direction of argument. He needed to gather his thoughts.

But was he right to criticise him considering his own actions with Georgina? Should he tell him what happened with her?

No.

She was the victim in all this. She should be kept out of it all and Patrick should suffer.

"Have you thought what this will do to Georgie and the kids?" Daniel asked.

"Nothing will happen."

"Wow." Daniel replied sarcastically. "For someone in your position, with a surprising amount of authority, you sure don't know how the world works do you?"

"And what do you mean by that?"

"Of course she's going to find out." Daniel said. "She's going to find out one way or the other and she's going to leave you and take the kids."

"She won't find out."

"How the hell are you so sure?" Daniel asked.

Patrick pensively looked out of the window. "I just know. I'm careful. I plan it all, and Helen can be trusted."

"She'll ditch you at the first opportunity when she sniffs someone better to help her in her career." Daniel said, recalling how he himself was treated by her.

Patrick looked over at him, "She wouldn't do that."

"No?"

"No! We - "

"Please don't say you love each other," Daniel said. "It's not love, but lust."

"And what would you know about it?" Patrick said harshly. "Look, this is my life, my situation, and you don't know shit about it. The only way Georgie is going to find out is if someone tells her. And I certainly won't. Helen won't, so that just leaves you."

Daniel turned the car into the final road and pulled it to a stop in the quiet street. He knew he couldn't and shouldn't tell Georgina about him, despite his feelings for her. To tell her would destroy her trust not only in Patrick, but also in Daniel for being the person who brought the devastation to her door. No, he would never tell her.

"If you're not going to tell her," Daniel said, "at least end it now."

Patrick gave a sly smile and shook his head. Why should he end it? He was happy, Georgina was happy in her belief of a stable marriage. He was comfortable with the deceit. "Sorry for not taking the advice of a divorced man." He said climbing out of the car and slamming the door shut.

Daniel could feel the anger welling up inside him and he swung the door open and emerged from the car. "Hey!" he shouted across the road. "I may be divorced, but I have a hell of a lot more experience in this than you."

"Oh really?"

Daniel ran his hands through his hair in exasperation. "My god you are so infuriating." He said. "What divine intervention suddenly makes you right about everything? What makes you think that you know best? You may be an Inspector, Paddy, but you are so insulated from the reality of the world, you think and see everything as black and white. You see yourself as a flag bearer for the moral stance the world should take, the lawful actions that we should all abide by.

"But this is the real world where we can't live by the strict rules. There is no black and white, and you believe in the system so much, you think your views and beliefs are the only ones that matter. You think that because you say something, then that's it, no more discussion and the world will fall into place behind you."

"You're talking crap!"

"You've done it all our lives." Daniel continued. "You think as the elder brother, you have the right to command and steer us, me and James, to the beliefs you hold so dear."

Patrick took a step into the road and faced him. "You don't know what you're talking about."

"There you go again." Daniel said mockingly, "That's your *belief*. But it's not mine. Just because you're the eldest doesn't mean you have the right to command us. Why do you think James contacted me about Anna? Why do you think I'm the point of contact for when he has an episode? Because we both know what you're like and you'd try to control things to suit your own mindset, and you would've probably told James to leave the Church and be a dad." Daniel threw his arms up in frustration. "You have never thought about the wants and desires of either of us, you've always gone after what suits you, and expected us to accept it."

Patrick took a slow step forward towards Daniel. "You've waited a long time to say that haven't you? Well let me retort for a moment, little brother. I have always tried to look out for you and Jimmy. I have always tried to be the brother that helps and supports his siblings, unlike you who phones me for help with his gambling debts. I may be stubborn in my views, but that's because of the unique position I see of the world. I see the true face of the world, the cruelty, the pain and suffering. You just write about it. So if my views seem arcane or old fashioned, it because they've been shaped by the influence of seeing the true nature of society, from the streets as a police officer. I know what I'm doing," he said. "I know what me and Helen have, and I know what me and Georgie don't have. I have something missing in my life and Helen fills it. I don't intend to be lectured by you about this."

"Don't go up there." Daniel said. "End it now. She will never be what you want her to be."

"And what's that then?" Patrick asked. "Give me your insight into my life."

Daniel looked hard at his brother. He had seen the true nature of Helen, had seen the side of her that his brother had not. "She's ambitious, probably why you're attracted to her, but that's all she is." He said. "She's a woman who'll use you for her own needs and then cast you aside. But you think it's love? You think she can add the thing that's missing from your life? You're mistaken. You may think that now, but she is not what you want her to be.

Patrick turned away from him and headed over to Helen's house.

"Paddy!" Daniel shouted. "For once, listen to someone else. Don't go back in there."

Patrick turned and looked at his brother in the street. "Go home Danny." He said, "Go home to your lonely life."

Daniel closed the door behind him and threw his keys onto the table as he slumped into his chair. It had been a few long emotional hours and on the drive home he had recounted the argument with Patrick.

He should've said more, he thought. *But what?*

Daniel closed his eyes and tried to rid the memory temporarily from his mind, and he sat and listened to the steady beat of the clock on the wall.

As he recounted the past few hours his mind retraced his own chequered past. He remembered the night he was working late at the newspaper offices in London and in the desk light glow he started talking to the new intern who had started working there a month before. She was just out of university, eager to learn and very easy on the eye.

He took her out to conferences and events to allow her to get a feel for the world of a reporter and that evening they sat and chatted about her future prospects. As he made them both drinks the conversation turned to the downside of the job, the long hours and strain it could have on relationships. It transpired that the girl, Stacey, was single.

There was something in the way she asked about his marriage that caused him to open up to her, telling her that things weren't good between him and Samantha at home.

She touched his arm and their hands brushed against each other.

As they fell onto the bed of the hastily booked hotel room, more of their flesh brushed each other and that night was the start of many nights together.

Daniel opened his eyes and grimaced. *How could he be so stupid and weak as to ruin his marriage?* He had hurt everyone he loved by making one stupid mistake. There had to be a way he could make sure Patrick didn't follow the traumatic path he had taken. There had to be a way to stop him from tearing his family apart.

CHAPTER 17

"We have CCTV!"

Patrick hung up the phone and headed into the main investigation office where his officers were gathered around a TV. The DVD recording of the CCTV from the home of Clive Lancashire came to life and the officers stood and watched it.

None of them had seen the footage before that moment, and Patrick, like the others around him he guessed, were feeling a mixture of excitement, anticipation and trepidation. It was the first possible lead the investigation had had, and he hoped it gave them something to go on.

A face and identification was the best scenario, but at that time, Patrick would've taken anything.

"What time did the driver drop him off?" Patrick asked. Although he knew the answer, having read the report half a dozen times already, he asked more to break the tense silence that had fallen on the office.

"About 10pm." An officer to his right said.

On the screen they watched as a black and white image of the driveway was shown. The gravelled in/out drive swept around the circle of grass in front of the house, and from the street lights casting long shadows over the grounds, they watched as the shadows started to move.

"That's the gate opening."

The footage showed the time as being 9:45pm, and on the screen a lone figure walked silently towards the door. Dressed in what appeared to be a long black coat, the figure's head was covered with a hood.

Everybody standing around the TV dared not move. The high acute angle of the camera above the front door showed the figure approach the house and ring the doorbell. It was immediately opened by Jessica Lancashire and the figure was let in. As the door closed, the police officers let out their collective breath.

At least they had something, Patrick thought.

"There was no struggle." One officer said. "No urgency or attack."

"He was let in." said another. "Those gates are what? Ten feet high? They were a security conscious couple, and they paid for the best. They must've known him."

"And the speed of her opening the door from him ringing the bell?" someone added. "It was as if she was expecting him."

"The 999 call recording does have Clive stating *You*. Said in a way that suggests he knows the attacker."

"Can we get SOCO to look at the intercom button and the doorbell. See what they can do?" Patrick asked. He sat on a desk and watched as the footage slowly ticked by, second by second. His mind could only imagine what was happening inside. His officers were right. It looked as though the attacker was known to the Lancashire couple, she had let the killer in.

So was that a link? Was the killer known to all of the victims?

"Can we do a background check on all of the victims so far and see if they overlap anywhere? Are they linked or have any known liaison with the others?" Patrick asked.

"Gaffer," one of the constables said, "SOCO on the phone, they want a word with you."

Patrick took the phone. "Inspector King."

"Boss, it's Michael Ferguson."

"Fergie, someone with some sense."

"I try." He said. *"They say you have CCTV footage and you want us to look at the intercom button and doorbell?"*

"Yes. The offender pressed the buttons, so we need to get the prints off the buttons and fast track them through."

There was a pause on the line and Ferguson thought. *"The probability of getting anything off them is close to zero."*

"This is the best lead we've got," Patrick said. "we need those prints."

"I understand that sir, but fingerprints on those items will be difficult."

"This is a murder investigation Fergie!" Patrick snapped.

"Forensic evidence doesn't just appear because you want it to be there. I know it's a murder, but the same techniques would be used as we would at a burglary or theft." Ferguson explained. *"And in the 15 years I've been doing this sir, I've never known anyone get a print off a doorbell."*

Patrick rubbed the bridge of his nose. While his major investigations relied heavily on the Forensics department, he was frustrated by their lack of co-operation in fulfilling his requests. Over the years he had had many arguments with different Crime Scene Managers from the forensics team who had refused his requests because they claimed they were almost impossible to achieve.

He had felt like banging his head against a wall, as on one hand the department would trumpet its own self importance of how great forensics could be, but then on the other they would cut short any possible lead that may be of some use.

He liked Ferguson, they had been out drinking and had worked on a few major jobs together. He appreciated his judgement and his forthcoming to say if something was worth doing or not. If Ferguson was saying it would be impossible, he had to trust his experience and knowledge.

Patrick needed a lead and he wasn't going to let this one slip away. "How about DNA?" he asked. "Can we get that?"

"There's a chance." Ferguson replied. *"But it will cost a fortune to get it tested. I mean, we're talking about touch-DNA, literally the smallest amount of contact between the finger and button."*

Money, Patrick thought. The other barrier he had to contend with. Sending the samples to an independent laboratory costs money, and while the forensics unit wouldn't pay it themselves, the investigation did have a budget of its own, granted through the powers of the higher echelons on the Force. He would have to get it authorised, but it was definitely worth a shot. "No expense spared," Patrick said. "Swab it and I'll get it paid for."

Ferguson agreed, but he could tell there was a reluctance in his voice about doing it.

Patrick handed the phone back to the officer as he watched a car emerge onto the screen. The officers re-assembled and watched Clive Lancashire climb out of the car, speak to his driver and then take his bags inside.

"What time is this now?"

"9:57 pm."

The minutes ticked past and as the time code passed the moment of the 999 call, the officers collectively leaned forward as they watched the man emerge from the house.

This is it! Patrick thought.

The man descended the steps onto the drive way and started to head back towards the gate. The image was grainy and it was difficult to make anything out, but they all strained their eyes to try and find any unique characteristic that could determine his identity.

The officer at the computer terminal clicked a button and the image changed to a wide angle shot of the grounds showing the curved driveway and the figure approaching the gates.

Another change in the camera angle overlooked the gates and the black figure moved through the opening gates. The officers watched as the hooded figure moved underneath the position of the camera and disappeared from view.

The disappointment within the office was palpable.

Patrick sat silently for a moment and looking around saw the despondency of his team. "OK. At least we have something. Get this over to Digital Forensics and see what they can do in enhancing it. See if they can get an estimate of height and build too. Compare that footage to anything else we have."

He could feel the energy returning to the team as they moved off back to their desks. "Speak to the driver," Patrick said, "see what he can tell us. And anyone else you can think of, neighbours, family, friends, gardener. Check the street for neighbouring houses and see if there are any other cameras. This is a posh area, there must be other camera's about."

He turned to head back to his office, when Helen caught his eye. "Can I have a word?" she asked.

He hadn't managed to speak to her properly since Daniel had dragged him from her house the previous night. On his return to her address he had only managed to pick up his keys when his mobile rang and had informed him of the double murder. Since that moment, he had been anxious to try and speak to her.

He closed the door behind her. "I need to speak to you too." He said. "Look, I'm sorry about last night. I don't know how Danny found me, but I'm embarrassed by it. He shouldn't have done it. There was a family issue, but still, it was out of order for him to do what he did."

"I understand," Helen said, "but that's not what I wanted to speak to you about." She handed him an envelope.

"What's this?"

Helen sat down in the spare seat. "There's an acting DI post on the Eastern side coming up. I'm going to apply for it, but I need a reference."

Patrick opened the letter and read it. "I hadn't heard of anything coming up." He said.

"I'm friends with the DCI over there," she said. "He gave me the head's up."

Patrick nodded and looked at her. "Yeah, I mean of course I'll write a glowing reference for you. You deserve the opportunity."

Helen gave a sigh of a relief and stood up. "Thanks. Just hope I get it."

Patrick smiled at her. "Of course you will. Positive thinking."

As she headed to the door, Patrick caught her up, placing his hand on hers. "About last night, I really am sorry."

"And I said don't worry about it." She said.

"Can I see you later?"

She paused and pulled her hand away from under his. "Perhaps we should calm things for a bit." She said. "Don't want to risk anything now Danny knows."

She was right of course and he nodded. She really would go far in the police, he thought as he stepped back and let her leave.

His thoughts for the next few moments were of Helen, the way she looked the night before, curled up on the sofa next to him. It felt safe, content, relaxed and perfect. He smiled to himself as he remembered the kissing, the touching, the love making.

With every second he was with her, the more he wanted to stay with her. He knew he had a decision to make about his future, and if he was totally honest with himself, he had made the decision and Helen Kolar was going to be in it.

*

"Bless me Father, for I have sinned."

The words were familiar, but with the low raspy voice, James found them chilling. He patiently waited for the penitent to continue his confession, but the man didn't continue, it was if he wanted prompting.

"Go ahead." James whispered, his own voice hoarse and dry.

"Father, the Lord spoke to me again and I was compelled to follow his command."

"Following the path laid down by God, is a righteous decision." James said.

"Righteous?" the man asked. *"Righteous men do righteous actions, for the good of all mankind."*

"And who do you do your actions for?"

"A vengeful God who sees evil in the world." The man said. *"I followed an angel to a house, I was welcomed inside where I found two souls who lived in the luxury of wealth that is beyond the reach of many men. I was sick to the stomach and I tried to focus my mind by reciting prayers. But -"*

James found himself leaning forward in the confessional booth, listening to the man. "Go ahead. You have nothing to fear here."

"But as I spoke the Lord's prayer, as I held the rosary in my hands, I saw visions of their deaths. I took the life of the woman first, and then the man, I fulfilled the prophecy that I saw."

"Do you feel guilty?"

"No." the man said simply. *"I feel thankful that the Lord God has given me the chance, chosen me to act for him. To strike fear into the world that has been long missing. Mankind has forgotten who created them, who brought life to this world. God created us all, he gave the foundations to build a world and to live upon it. It was the greatest gift he could bestow upon us, and how do we repay him – by living and manipulating a world that no longer recognizes the power and leadership of the church.*

"Youngsters go about worshipping those persons within the media, those self-serving persons who only seek wealth and fame. I look around and I see the people trying desperately to reach for wealth they shouldn't need or want. Greed is a curse, an evil that will consume the soul. Lust corrupts the heart, and the betrayal of one's emotions erode the loyalty to those we love. Sloth shows the lowest levels that man can tread."

James listened intently to the man. "You must resist the urges and try to contain your behaviour. God will understand if you refuse. He will see your strength."

"My strength is in my willing to continue his desires."

"More people may get hurt." James said.

"I assure you, they will." The man said. He recited the Act of Contrition and James could only listen as he blessed the man and absolved him of his sins.

Certain that the man had left the booth, James leaned back and ran his hands through his hair. He was listening to the confessions a of a killer, and there was nothing he could do. He was bound by his oath of the Sacrament of

Confession never to reveal or disclose what had been said. The oath had been practiced by generations of priests throughout history, and as much as he knew he should pass the information on, James couldn't bring himself to break the oath he had sworn to uphold.

He crossed himself and left the booth, stepping out into the dimly lit church. He walked towards the altar and casting a look at the complete nativity scene in the Sacred Heart chapel to the left of the main altar. He found solace in the scene, hope and love. His mind calmed as he looked at the images of Mary, Joseph, the Shepherds and the Wise Men as they patiently and silently waited for the arrival of Jesus into their world.

As he passed the pews, he saw a few parishioners kneeling and praying and as he passed the final row, he looked over to see someone he would never thought of seeing in Church.

Daniel looked up at him. "I think I need some advice."

CHAPTER 18

There was something about the way he made his cups of coffee, Daniel thought. There was always the right amount of sugar, the milk was the perfect quantity, the ratios were always to perfection.

"Six stirs anti-clockwise," James would say, *"six clockwise, then one anti-clockwise and a tap of the spoon on the side."*

Whatever his secret, it worked every time.

Daniel sipped the drink and followed James into the sitting room. He had started to talk about Anna, telling him that he and Patrick had spoken to her and she had agreed not to demand the two thousand pounds from him. Daniel refrained from telling him that he had threatened her with reporting her to social services. He knew James would disapprove, but he knew the lie was better than the truth.

When Anna had first approached James saying she was pregnant, he was adamant that he would try his hardest to support her and his child. Daniel, although he disagreed with his decision, he had told James not to give money to her directly. Daniel had therefore set up a separate account for James to deposit money each month, and Anna would have access to it whenever she needed it.

Now that Anna had been cut off from that money, Daniel had worked out that the money would remain in the account for the coming years and become a small savings for him. Knowing his brother though, he would probably donate it to charity.

They sat down in the comfortable high backed chairs. "Thank you for helping with Anna." James said. "It affected me more than I thought it would."

"Don't mention it," Daniel replied, "you'd do the same for me."

James shifted in his seat. "Speaking of which?"

Daniel smiled, "Yeah, thought we'd have to get to that sooner or later."

"So what's bothering you?"

Daniel had to take a breath. He didn't really know where to start. There was so much going through his head with the loss of his job, the argument with Patrick, and the kiss with Georgina. He wanted to share it all, but there were things he wanted to keep to himself.

The kiss.

It was so special, so intimate and passionate, that it had played on his mind since the moment he had left her alone. He had had a text from her: THINKING OF YOU xx; but he hadn't replied. He didn't know how to.

He wanted to tell her that he was thinking of her too, like he had been thinking of her for the majority of his life, but he couldn't bring himself to send it.

Why not??

He had asked himself the question every time he typed out the message, but then something made him delete it. Her husband was cheating on her, she was lonely, needing of attention, and he was willing to give it.

Was it honour? Loyalty to Patrick? Guilt?

He didn't know, but he wished he could make a decision and act on it.

"Where do I start?" he said. "I guess losing my job is playing on my mind. Getting screwed over by the owner's son was a kick in the balls."

"Are they still churning up the past?"

Daniel nodded. "Like you wouldn't believe."

James looked at his brother, watching as he took a sip of his drink. He had seen the look in his eyes and face before and had also seen Daniel fight the inner turmoil of his demons before. James remembered when he had confessed about his affairs to him, and his final acceptance of his gambling addiction. Daniel would be quiet, contemplating his own situation, as if almost debating whether or not to share it with his brother. "But what's really on your mind?" James pressed.

"Me and Paddy had a run in." Daniel said finally.

James nodded slowly. Over the years he had seen and heard his brothers argue and fall out. He had seen their rivalry throughout their childhood, and at times watched as it had boiled over, sometimes in physical fights.

While some of their fighting stemmed from their personality similarities, other times it came from their differences. Daniel was a dreamer, a young man who would plan for the future, make plans and set himself goals; while Patrick was more likely to focus on today.

James remembered how there came a time when Patrick was needed to make a decision on the path his life was to take, he needed a career. With a degree in maths, he had toyed with the idea of training to be a teacher, but instead, he chose to apply to join the police.

When he told his family his plans, Daniel didn't try to hide the disappointment on his face. Since he had been 6 years old, he had wanted to be a police officer. He watched the cop shows, read books, practiced the entry exams 3 years before he was eligible to take them. With his naturally skilled observational abilities, everybody thought he would be a perfect police officer.

He had worked hard at school to try and prepare himself for joining, but as soon as he had heard Patrick's proclamation of his new *desire* to join the police, Daniel had dropped out of his extra classes, and started to take long walks alone.

Patrick had stolen his dreams, and James knew Daniel would've called upon Georgina to walk with him, to talk about things, to try and formulate and forge a new path, so close the two of them were. But again, Patrick had moved his own attention onto her, pushing Daniel out, and allowing his own relationship with her to develop.

Daniel had resented Patrick since those moments for what he considered to be stealing his dreams, hopes, and girl, but Patrick didn't see the wrong he had done. He had found a future to work for, and despite his brother's protestations, he continued to follow Daniel's chosen path.

They had argued about it over the years, and Patrick rebuked what he called the false accusations of his younger brother, telling him to find his own life and to stop trying to live his. He had brushed Daniel away and arrogantly continued to walk proudly, believing he had done no wrong, when in his wake, there was turmoil, upset, and pain.

James looked at his brother sitting opposite him and saw that the years of hurt were starting to take their toll on him. "Dare I ask what happened?"

Daniel looked away, not wanting to tell his brother about Patrick's secret. But it was a burden that was gnawing away at him, and he knew he couldn't keep hold of it much longer.

"Do you remember," Daniel said slowly, "why my marriage broke down?"

James nodded. "Yes."

"I think – hell – I know, Paddy's on the same path." Daniel said. "I don't know how long it's been going on, but he's going to ruin his marriage."

James was silent for a moment, holding his hands beneath his chin. "It's his life." He said finally, "Let him live it."

Daniel closed his eyes, trying to choose the words. "But – he'll ruin everything. His marriage, his family."

"Tell me," James said, "are you truly more worried about Patrick, or Georgina?"

Daniel looked at him. "What do you mean?"

James leaned forward and looked into his brother's eyes. "Danny, I see how you look at her, I see there are still feelings there for her. I see it every time we're all together. The longing in your heart, the desire to be with her. I see it, Patrick obviously doesn't given his narrow view of the world, but Georgie sees it too."

Daniel sat back hard and roughly put his cup on the side.

"Danny! I had to ask." James said quickly seeing the frustration in him. "But you do don't you?"

It was as though the words were caught in his throat. *James could see it? Georgina could see it too?* "Yes." He said finally, "But I've known her for years, of course I have feelings for her. I worry about her and the kids, I don't want to see her hurt."

James sat back and looked away. There was so much he wanted to say, so much he knew he couldn't say so as to appear he was preaching. He had always been upset that Daniel's marriage had broken down, and he thought that Patrick would've seen the pain it had caused, but obviously he was wrong.

"You can't pursue her." James said.

"What – what do you mean?"

"Georgie." James explained. "You can't pursue her. If their marriage is in difficulty, the best thing we can do is let them work it out."

"But I could help." Daniel said.

"No – no you couldn't." James replied. "I may not be as worldly knowledgeable as you, but if you try to pursue her, you'll make things worse for them – for her. Their marriage will be over and you'll be the cause of it, and she'll resent you for it."

"So you're saying -"

"Wait." James said. "Wait and let them try and work it out."

Daniel let the words sink in and he looked at James. "Are you, as a priest, telling me to wait before I covet my brother's wife?"

James gave a small smile, but there was no humour there. "I know what he's like." He said. "I know his faults, I've seen him over the years take people for granted, and pushed them away once he's used them. He promised me he wouldn't do this again."

"What?" Daniel said, the shock evident. "What?? Are you saying he's had an affair before?"

"Four years ago."

Daniel closed his eyes, bit his lip and shook his head slowly. He couldn't believe it. "Bastard."

"Daniel!" James snapped.

"Sorry, but he is."

James gave him a questioning look.

"Yes, I know the irony of that." Daniel said smiling.

A silence fell between them and they both sat back listening to the steady second hand of the clock on the mantelpiece. A peace fell upon them both, and with the warmth of the house falling like a blanket, Daniel could feel the stress of the past few days start to catch up with him. There was something comforting about the house, something serene, and he started to understand why James, when he was younger would run off the Abbey, to find a quiet place to gather his thoughts.

For the first time in days was calm, and he could feel the tension begin to lift from his mind and shoulders. It was true, he thought, sharing problems made them appear smaller and less intimidating than keeping them to yourself.

It was too tempting and easy to sit there and fall asleep, but he knew he should head home. He couldn't use the safety of James's parochial house to hide away in. He needed to head home.

"I should go." He said.

James was feeling the tiredness too and he walked Daniel to the door. "Think about what I said. They have their problems, let them work it out."

Daniel knew he was right, and he wished his heart would allow him to follow his advice. "I will." He lied.

"And don't worry about work." James said. "God always has a plan, let his wisdom guide you. Something will always work out. Remember what mother used to say."

"It'll all come out in the wash." Daniel quoted, smiling. "Thanks little brother."

"My door is always open."

"As is mine."

James watched Daniel walk down to his car. He hoped Daniel would heed his advice. He would hate to see Patrick's marriage fall apart, but to see it fall apart because of Daniel would be a wound upon the family that nothing, not even time could heal.

CHAPTER 19

Georgina sat at the counter as Clarissa and Charlie ate their breakfast, watching their morning television programmes. As the over enthusiastic presenters jumped around trying to get the zombified children of the nation active, she wondered first of all how they could have so much energy, and then why they were getting children so excited, 10 days before Christmas.

She sipped her tea as the familiar theme tune of the excruciatingly annoying show started. She blocked out the noise as she thought back to those intimate moments with Daniel. She had found herself thinking about them at any spare moment she had, and instead of being horrified with herself for what she had done, she found herself smiling at the memory.

He had a tender touch, his lips were soft and his breath was warm. As he kissed her neck, it was like sparks were tingling throughout her body as she sensed the passion within him to be with her. And she knew she wanted to be with him too.

As she heard the front door close, signalling the arrival home of her husband, she knew the hypocrisy of what she had done, and the accusations she was about to throw at her husband. He had lied to her before, and she knew he would lie to her now. His deception far outweighed her own, so no, she thought, he would suffer the full accusations she was ready to throw at him.

As Patrick entered the kitchen, she looked up at him and without asking, he started with his excuse.

"Sorry," he said. "but we've got new leads to follow and time just got away from us."

"You could've called." She said, not wanting the frustration or emotion to show in her voice in front of the children.

"It was late." Patrick said, as calmly as he could appear to be as he made himself a drink.

"I didn't know where you were, you should've known I was worried. It doesn't matter what time, you should've called."

"I'm sorry," Patrick said, with more frustration in his voice than he intended. "I will next time."

Georgina rolled her eyes slightly and turned away from him. She had heard all of his excuses before. The working late, the *major job* and the *new leads*. She knew he was leading a major investigation, but she wished he could prioritise things better.

But, however much she tried to believe he was really working late into the night *following new leads*, there was no denying the distinct smell of woman's perfume on him.

She thought she had noticed it a week or so before, but had dismissed it as her imagination. But with each passing day and each pitiful excuse, the more she saw through his lies. She could no longer look him in the eyes.

"Dad," Charlie said. "Will Santa get my letter in time?"

Patrick looked as though he had only just noticed Charlie and he knelt next to him. "Have you written it?"

Charlie handed him a long list of presents.

"Wow!" Patrick said. "Have you been a good boy?"

"Always."

"Then I'm sure Santa could sort something out."

Georgina interrupted them both. "Come on you two, go and get dressed and washed, we've got things to do today."

As Clarissa and Charlie left the kitchen, Patrick looked at the Christmas lists of both his children. "I don't even recognise half of the things they want on here. What happened to good old Lego?"

"Don't worry," Georgina said shortly, "It's been sorted. As it always is."

Patrick threw the pages down and looked at his wife. He thought he had detected the tone of her voice before, but had ignored it, but this time, there was no disguising it. "What does that mean?"

She picked up the dirty cups, dishes and cutlery. "It's another Christmas where I've been left to sort it all out. Not just my family, the kids, but yours too."

"I told you not to do my side." Patrick said, "I'll do it."

"When? When would you do it?" She asked. "You can't even find time to come home and spend time with your kids. You missed their nativity play, and end of year party. You're absorbed so much in your world that you forget about us and don't pay us any attention."

"It's work." Patrick said. "I need to do my work."

"It's a woman!" Georgina snapped.

Silence.

Patrick looked at her, trying to keep his face as neutral as possible. He wanted to look impassive, natural, as innocent as he could. He tried to remember the tells his arrested suspects would give to indicate their guilt or not. The eye contact, too little or too much either would make him look guilty. Where should his arms be? Across his chest is a barrier, too loose to the side and he opens himself up for attack. He tried to remember the best way to act.

"Well?" Georgina asked.

"What?"

Georgina shook her head, smiling in frustration, and continued to fill the dishwasher. "If I was a cop, I'd say you were guilty by your lack of response. Why not go *No Comment* and make it official?"

"There is no other woman." Patrick said, feeling his face begin to flush and voice crackle. "There isn't."

"I wish I could believe you," She said. "But I can't." She added as she slammed the dishwasher door, rattling the items inside.

Patrick was in disbelief. He knew he could either stand his ground and deny every accusation she could throw at him, or simply admit it. Admit the affair.

In his mind, he had foreseen the moment of telling her as more controlled, on his terms, when he was ready. He had never thought of the possibility of near enough being ambushed like this. He wanted to be in a position where he could tell her, and make her see that his decisions were the best for them both. He wanted to show her while he still loved her, he needed time to himself to gather his thoughts and emotions and then he could come back to her, and their relationship would be stronger.

He had to make a decision, there was no chance to weigh up the options and have an internal debate. He had to act on impulse, and face the accusations head on, something he knew he wasn't used to doing.

"Did Danny tell you?" he asked quietly.

"What? Daniel? Why the hell would Daniel tell me?" she asked, and then paused, thinking, and suddenly realising. "He knew didn't he. Was that why he came round here the other night looking for you?" She forced a laugh, but it lacked humour. "Jesus, does your whole family lie?"

"Georgie -"

"Don't!" she snapped, facing him and throwing a cup, missing him by inches. Tears were rolling down her face, the emotion was too overwhelming. "I can't take any more of your lies." She wiped the tears from her face and forced a smile. "This was meant to be a great Christmas, us, James, Daniel, my parents, all of us together for the first time in years. But you've gone and screwed it up because you couldn't keep your dick in your trousers."

"I'm sorry." Patrick said feebly.

"You promised!" Georgina cried. "After last time you promised you wouldn't do this again. You stood right there and you promised me!"

Patrick was struggling for words. He thought when it all came out, it would be easier than this. He envisaged standing strong and tall and telling her it was over. But now he realised he wanted to try and calm her, apologise and stay with her.

The sudden realisation of where his heart truly belonged opened up to him. Despite his previous thoughts, he could see the hurt his actions were having on his wife, and the guilt rushed over him. He was now faced with the diminishing future of losing everything. "I don't know what to say." He said simply.

Georgina dried her face and crossed her arms, avoiding his eyes. "Well I have to get the kids ready. When you've thought of something – tell it to somebody who cares. In fact," she turned and grabbed her coat from the chair, "you sort the kids out. I'm going out."

She turned from him and left the kitchen.

"Can I stay here?" he asked meekly.

"Do what you want," she replied over her shoulder. "you appear to do that anyway, but you won't be sleeping in our bed tonight."

*

Daniel stood in his kitchen and started to stir his coffee. *How did James do it again? Six clockwise, six anti-clockwise, and a tap of spoon on the side?*

He tried to recall the instructions and tasted the coffee. No, he hadn't got it right, he thought as he shook his head. "Must be the intervention of God." He said to himself, smiling at his own joke.

He heard a knock on the front door and answered it to see Colin Parker, he ex-editor, standing before him. Daniel was surprised to see him there and it took him a few seconds to gather his thoughts.

"Aren't you going to let me in?" Colin asked.

Daniel regained his composure and stepped to the side to let him pass. In the living room Colin took the offer of a seat and declined a cup of coffee.

"Good job," Daniel said, taking his seat in the armchair, " it tastes like crap. So," he continued, "I'm guessing this isn't a social call. How're Marcus Book and that moron, Evans was it?"

Colin rolled his eyes as he slumped into a chair. "Oh god, Evans is sticking his oar in at every possibility. I'm sure he thinks he could run the paper better than Jesus himself. I've had more run-ins with him than I care to remember, and he thinks he's Marcus Book's right hand man. Every time someone stands up to him, it's the same old response of *'Mr. Book will hear of this.'*. I swear I almost decked him the other day."

"So a normal day in the office then?" Daniel asked sarcastically.

"You could say that."

"So why are you here?" He asked, sipping his coffee.

Colin leaned forward, his arms on his knees. "We all know Marcus Book knows sod-all about the newspaper industry and what sells newspapers, but unfortunately it's the one thing he wants. More copies sold. He thinks to sell papers, you need young girls with their nips out on every other page and gossip wrangling crap stories about some has-been celebrity nobody cares about. He doesn't care about the real stories out there and only wants the tabloid crap."

"That is a pickle, you're in." Daniel said, finding it easy to act as if he didn't care what happened.

"The thing is Danny," Colin continued as if he hadn't heard him, "we know, both of us, that newspapers need to report the real stories too. We shouldn't be treating the readers like yobs and bullish football thugs who only care about tits and sport. We need real stories reported."

Daniel looked at his ex-boss and shrugged. "Yeah, well, that's why you have a newsroom full of journalists."

"But none of them are as good as you."

"Can't argue there." Daniel said, toasting him with his mug and a smile.

"What I'm saying is, we've got the biggest police investigation in a generation going on right in our city, and our articles so far are written like a child has done them. They're regurgitating the facts and nothing is original. I swear they plagiarised something the other day from one of the national papers. If the lawyers find out, we're screwed."

Daniel stood up, with half an idea of knowing where the conversation was going. "So – you need help."

"Yes."

The men looked at each other, and Daniel waited for the question, but it never came. "Ask me dammit!"

"I thought I had."

"My god, for an editor you have a crap way with words."

Colin laughed. "Danny, I need you to work on this murder story. Use your knowledge, contacts, do whatever it is you do to get me a story."

"Marcus Book won't like it."

"Screw him." Colin said. "You can be a consultant, or some other made up name."

Daniel paced slowly around his living room, thinking. *Did he really want to do their hard work for them? Did he really want to investigate the murders, and in effect, go head to head against his brother?*

Yes. He knew the answer before he asked himself the question.

"I'll do it." He said after a moment's silence. "When do I start?"

"Did you ever finish?" Colin said smiling and standing up.

Daniel grinned and shook his hand. "I'll see what I can do."

"Email me when you have something." Colin said as he headed to the door.

Daniel listened as the door opened and closed. This was just what he needed, he thought. Something to focus on and allow his mind to work on. He had to admit he needed something to keep his mind off Patrick, James and most of all Georgina.

He turned from the window and suddenly saw Georgina standing before him.

"That man let me in." she said.

"That was nice of him." Daniel said, taking a step towards her. "Can I -"

He never finished his sentence as her hand whipped around and slapped him hard across the cheek. "You bastard!" she said.

CHAPTER 20

"Normally I know what I've done when a woman slaps me like that." Daniel said, rubbing his cheek. The sizzling pain was easing as he moved his jaw.

Georgina ignored him and took her coat off throwing it on the sofa. He could tell she was angry, could tell she was upset, and he had a pretty good idea he knew about what. He didn't need his observational skills to read her behaviour.

"You knew?" she asked. "You bloody knew and you said nothing to me?"

Daniel was on the defensive and he held his hands up. "Just wait there, missy." He said, "First of all – hello – and second of all, what the hell are you on about?"

"Don't play dumb with me, you're a smart person."

Daniel smiled, "Actually most of the time I am dumb, I just play at being smart." He said, trying to relax and calm the situation.

"Patrick?!" Georgina spat. "You knew about him screwing around?"

Daniel took a breath and let it out slowly. "Yes." He answered finally. "I had an idea that something was going on."

"Why didn't you say something?"

"I wanted to -"

"Why didn't you?" she interrupted.

"If you give me a chance to answer," he said forcefully, "I'll tell you!"

Georgina slumped into the sofa as Daniel spoke. It was as though her strength had dissipated and she had no energy. "I suspected something was going on the other night," Daniel said, "but how was I meant to bring it up? How would that conversation start? I've been in turmoil for days, thinking about the effects it would have on you and the kids. How it would possibly end your marriage, and how you'd think of me." He sat down next to her. "Georgie, I haven't stopped worrying about the consequences this would have for you, and, selfishly, I didn't want you to associate me with this revelation. I didn't want you to look at me and hate me and think *'He's the one who told me!'*"

Georgina looked over at him, the tears flowing over her cheeks again. "You knew the other night? When you came over?"

He nodded. "I came over to speak to Patrick about it, confront him about my suspicions, but I didn't know for certain until later." He paused for a moment. "How did you find out?"

"I could smell it on him when he came in." she said, sniffing back the tears. "He was apparently working late, again, but I'd called his office around midnight and they said he had left an hour before."

"I'm sorry." Daniel said. He didn't know what else to say. He knew what he wanted to say, but it wasn't right for the situation. He wanted to tell her that his brother was a fool, that she should leave him, and that they should start a new life together. He wanted to tell her his feelings for her had grown, and that he wanted to act on them, but he knew he shouldn't.

"Don't be." She replied. "It's not your fault. And do you know the stupid thing? I've been more angry with you than I was with him."

"Yeah," Daniel said. "I bring out the anger in all people."

Georgina laughed and wiped her face dry. "God I must look terrible."

"You look fine. Coffee?"

They entered the kitchen and Daniel made two cups of coffee. They stood opposite each other, Daniel watched her over the lip of his mug. She was beautiful, he thought. There was a natural beauty that didn't need to be highlighted or artificially enhanced by make-up. She was amazing as she was right there.

"So what are you going to do?" he asked.

"God, I have no idea." She said. "He promised me last time that it wouldn't happen again, but I guess he thought he could get away with it this time. What can I do?"

Daniel had thought about it, and despite his feeling for her, and his desire to be with her, he knew his obligations as a brother. "Try not to do anything before Christmas." He said. "For the sake of Clarissa and Charlie. Let them enjoy the day and not have it associated with their parents splitting up."

"I don't know if I can stay in the same room as him."

Daniel shrugged. "It's him who should be trying to make things right. Let him do the hard work."

There was another silence between them, a tension, and Georgina took a sip of her drink. "This coffee tastes like shit by the way." She said bluntly.

Daniel smiled and laughed. "I know. I was trying to replicate James's coffee."

"Oh god, he makes good coffee." She agreed. "Must be the influence of God or something."

They laughed again and Daniel led her back into the living room and they sat down once more. "I'm sorry." He said again.

"What for?"

Daniel sheepishly avoided her eyes. "For not telling you."

She placed a hand on his arm. "You did the right thing. You shouldn't have. You were right, I would've blamed you and that's not fair on you." She looked at him, catching his eye and stroking his cheek where she had hit him. "I wasn't really angry at you." She said. "Guess it was all of a release."

"And I'm sorry about the other night." He said. "Between us."

She looked at him. "I'm not." She said. "It was nice. Comfortable. Exciting."

Daniel smiled. "I wanted to call you."

"I wanted you to call." She replied. "But – maybe it's better you didn't."

Daniel reluctantly nodded and placed his cup next to hers. "But maybe I should've." He said.

Georgina looked him in the eyes, and found herself staring into them. He stared back, taking in every detail of her face and lips.

As they kissed, their hands once more explored each other, and as the passion grew between them, the tension was released. The memories of the day disappeared and they wrapped themselves up in each other's body.

*

There was too much going on in his head for Patrick to really focus on things. He had brought Charlie and Clarissa to James' church to allow Charlie to practice his role as an altar server on Christmas Eve.

Seeing how excited Charlie was, and how attentive he was to the instructions of Fr. William, Patrick started to feel more at ease and some of the stress release from him. He started to try and put things in his mind into some sort of order.

The Church was decorated for the coming celebrations, and with the candles and quietness of the building, he thought about Georgina.

She had every right, he knew, to be angry with him. He had broken his promise to her and for that he would curse himself. But he didn't know if he was angry at himself for breaking the promise, or for getting found out. He looked up at the huge crucifix hanging above the main altar. Seeing the representation of the dying Christ, he found himself acknowledging he was angry about being found out.

Was he really like those other unfaithful men?

Did he want the perfect family set-up at home with a doting wife and children, but then the mistress to satisfy his sexual urges? He bowed his head, he knew the answer.

He did want that. But he knew he also wanted more.

His marriage with Georgina had become routine, the same, with the same problems and the same day to day tasks. Feed the kids, take them to school, go to work, pick them up, help with homework, have tea, watch TV, go to bed and then do it all again the following day.

It was monotonous, and Patrick had had enough of it. He had found someone who made his pulse race quicker, who was exciting and forceful. She knew what she wanted and wasn't afraid to ask for it, in and out of the bedroom.

Perhaps he shouldn't see the argument with Georgina as the beginning of the end, but the start of a new chapter where he finds happiness with someone he knew he loves more than his wife.

As he sat and watched Charlie walk through the steps of assisting during the Eucharist section of the Mass with Fr. William, and Clarissa admiring the Nativity Scene, James sat in the pew in front of him. "He's excited." He said, nodding at Charlie.

Patrick nodded. "I don't know if he's more excited about this or Christmas Day itself."

"I miss those days." James said. "The excitement of Christmas morning."

"I don't miss those jumpers mum made us one year." Patrick replied, smiling at the memory of the thick, ill-fitting, woollen tastelessly designed jumpers.

"Or the year the turkey was undercooked and raw in the middle?"

They both laughed at the image of seeing their father slice into the turkey to find the meat uncooked. They had sat around the table, worried expressions on their faces, expecting their father to raise his voice and lash out at them with his short temper, but instead, their father laughed out loud and fell back into his chair. Instead of turkey, they managed to collate nibbles and snacks for the rest of the festive season and as a family, sat on the floor in front of the open fire eating crisps, nuts, cheese and crackers.

Both of them felt it was the most relaxed and enjoyable Christmas either of them had had.

"Are you set for this year?" James asked.

Patrick let the smile drop away from his face. "So I've been told."

James could sense the edginess in his voice, the hidden subtext, and given what Daniel had told him, he had a good idea that Patrick and Georgina had had an argument, probably about his affair.

"Have you spoken to Danny yet?" James asked.

Patrick could feel himself tense up at the mention of his brother's name. "No, and I'm not really in the mood to talk to him."

"He needs us." James said.

Patrick scoffed at the comment. "He doesn't need anyone. He only cares about himself."

"Is that what you think?"

Patrick shot him a hard look. "It's true."

"Was he thinking of himself when he came to help me? When he helped with my – issues?"

"That was different." Patrick said.

"How?"

Patrick shrugged, trying to find an answer. "It was – I don't know, it was different because you're his brother."

"So are you."

"Oh please!" Patrick protested. "I know me and him have never seen eye to eye, but he has never put himself out for me. Not once, not even after I helped him with his gambling debts or the four grand he owed the bank." He said. He felt as though all of his brother's own vices should be voiced and reminded of, if his own indiscretions were to be publically admonished. No, Patrick wasn't perfect, but then neither was his brother.

"He saved your career." James said calmly.

"When?"

James wasn't sure he should tell Patrick, but then, he thought it could be the best thing to do to help them resolve their difficulties. "These last few weeks. He lost his job because of the internal investigation going on at the paper."

"When? For what?"

James didn't know all of the details, but explained what he knew regarding Daniels meeting about the information scandal between the newspapers and police, and the story of the son of the papers owner, Calum Book and his drug dealing arrest.

"That's why he was fired?" Patrick asked.

"From what I can gather, it was a combination of things, but I imagine it's because of the owner's son." James said. "His daddy didn't take too kindly to have his son exposed like that so Danny got fired. But the official reason couldn't be for that, so they used the scandal about passing information to the police as the cover story, and in doing so bringing an end to it all, and protecting you."

Patrick ran his hands through his hair, and resisted the urge to swear. He was himself facing difficulties at work from his Superintendants and if it was true now Daniel was no longer an accredited journalist, things could move on for the better. There wouldn't be the continual checking of information and reminders not to speak to the press.

Had Daniel really sacrificed himself for the good of him?

From the altar, Fr. William called for James, who excused himself and left Patrick alone.

"Goddamn it Danny." He said to himself. *Had Daniel in a long round-about way, managed to save Patricks career?*

He had never wanted Daniel to lose his job, or to get into trouble over his actions, but he couldn't believe the self-sacrifice he had made for the good of Patrick's career. And as much as he hated to acknowledge it, James was correct in his assumption that Daniel was always there for his brothers. He had been there for James; he had tried to help Patrick with Helen, but he hadn't listened; and when he thought about it, Daniel had always offered help to those around him.

But now, Daniel was alone and there was nobody in a position to help him.

What would Daniel do? Patrick thought.

He sat for a moment in silence, and then decided he had to do something to help him. He had to try and make it right, in the same way Daniel had tried and succeeded in helping James with Anna. He would go and speak to the man who had caused him to lose his job, and try and get him to take Daniel back.

DAVID WHELAN

PART FOUR

GLUTTONY

194

CHAPTER 21

The penthouse apartment overlooked the sprawling metropolis, and as the sun dipped beneath the horizon, the other face of the city, the nightlife began to emerge.

Calum Book stood at the floor to ceiling, double height window. Taking a sip from his wine glass, he admired the beauty of the streets and buildings, 25 storeys beneath him.

He turned from the window and walked over the polished tiled floors that he had personally chosen when his father had paid for the accommodation. He was used to and wanted the best of everything, and when the internal designer had sat down with him, Calum had ignored the colours, and pointed at the most expensive. He didn't care about the colours and how they worked with each other or about the karma and energy flow of the apartment. He wanted the expensive items, not because he needed them or they looked appropriate, but because he could afford them.

That, he believed, was why he, or rather his father, was paying the designer, to make it all work together.

Standing in front of a large gold framed mirror, Calum poured himself another drink and admired himself in his designer shirt, Italian designer trousers, and expensive shoes. He estimated the clothes he had on now were more than most people's monthly income. He gently moved his hand over his perfectly manicured hair, and he smiled at his reflection, showing off the perfectly constructed dental work.

With the right people, personal trainers, dental hygienists, and at least 6 holidays a year to various climates and high-end resorts, he saw himself as the epitome of what money could do for the body and soul.

People would work hard all their lives for this, he thought, but he knew he would never have to as his father paid for his lifestyle.

The heavy gold watch hung from his wrist as he sat on the custom made white leather sofa. On the coffee table before him were several small clear plastic packets, the powdered contents of which were lined up neatly before him.

He had already taken one hit of the drugs that day, but he thought he would treat himself to another before heading down town and picking up a drunk gaggle of women to bring back to the penthouse for a private party.

Money gets you everything, he thought as he leaned forward and inhaled the powder through a straw and up into his nose. With a week to go before the festivities, it really would be a *white* Christmas, he smiled to himself.

The hit was instant and he felt his whole body relax.

He had everything he wanted, he thought. Money, cars, women, city penthouse, drink, and as much drugs as he needed. He was living the dream.

Patrick read the address again and checked the building name and number, he was in the right place. The building was a monolithic giant in the centre of the city. With the bottom two thirds of the 25 storeys dedicated to a prestigious hotel chain, the remaining upper floors had been converted to apartments and penthouses for the super-rich.

As he pressed the buzzer and waited for a reply, Patrick was under no illusion that the penthouse had been paid for by Calum Book's father. "Rich bastard." He said just as the buzzer was answered.

"Yeah?"

Patrick held up his police ID to the camera, "Detective Chief Inspector King. May I have a quick word?"

Calum leered in close to the screen next to the phone.

The police? *Shit!*

His voice was slurring as he spoke, the effects of the drugs taking hold of his body and mind. "Er – yeah – okay." He said.

He held down the buzzer and let the officer into the building. Heading back into the living area of the penthouse, Calum quickly rubbed down the coffee table, trying to get rid of the evidence. *How much had that cost him?*

Didn't matter, he would claim compensation from the police from whatever false accusations they were about to throw at him, and buy some more, he thought.

There was a knocking at the front door.

Shit, he was quick!

Wiping the remainder of the drugs from his hands on his trousers, Calum headed to the door and tried to calm his breathing. He took a breath and opened the door.

He only saw the flash of the blade as it slashed across his field of view at the last minute. He tried to move out of the way, but the blade sliced into his hand cutting him deep.

Calum recoiled, but the attacker swung again, slashing up and cutting him deep into his back.

Given the amount of money the residents were paying for the apartments, you'd think they'd change the elevator music, Patrick thought.

He watched the numbers on the panel as they increased slowly to his destination.

He had no idea what he was going to say to Calum Book. *Could he threaten him like Daniel had done with Anna? Was he about to risk his career for his brother? Could he do that?*

As he drove to the penthouse he had reasoned answers for all of the questions, but as he neared his destination, he was starting to have doubts. He wanted to talk to him, to try and persuade him to allow Daniel to have his job back. But was he justified or right to try that?

With all his money and wealth, power and connections, Calum Book wouldn't be such an easy push over as Anna was, but he knew he had to try.

As the numbers slowly climbed, Patrick was thinking of an opening line he could use to try and gain some sort of rapport with Book.

Could he ask about the murders? Could he tell him there was a burglary in the building and he wanted to see if Calum had seen anything?

Questions and scenarios raced through his mind and finally as the elevator signalled his arrival, they all disappeared as he headed to the penthouse door.

Calum crawled away from his attacker, he could feel the blood pouring from his wounds, but the hooded man continued to advance on him. He tried to pull his mobile phone from his pocket, but the attacker carefully and purposefully stepped on his wrist, causing him to shout out in pain.

"Hello?" came a voice from the entrance hall.

The attacker looked towards the source of the voice and then back at Calum. This wasn't how it was meant to happen.

Leaving Calum bleeding on the floor, the hooded man headed towards the bedroom, to await his new prey.

"Hello?" Patrick called again as he carefully pushed the door open. He saw the blood marks on the door, and he stepped into the penthouse.

What the hell has happened? He thought as he saw the blood on the wall. "Police!" he called out. "Is anyone here?"

He wished he had his protective equipment with him for defence, but as a Detective Chief Inspector, he had to admit it had been few years since he had needed it. He pulled his mobile phone from his pocket and dialled *999*.

With it to his ear, he carefully followed the blood smears on the wall and floor and as the operator came on the line, he spoke quickly. "Detective Chief Inspector King, I need police assistance and an ambulance." He said, passing them the address.

As he rounded the corner of the hallway, he saw the bloodied body of Calum Book. "Get the ambo here now!" he shouted down the phone. "Male, multiple stab wounds, barely conscious and breathing."

As he knelt on the floor next to Calum, he could see the shallow dips of his chest, but they were getting weaker. Patrick was in shock at the scene, and his mind was awash with actions to take. His priority was to preserve life, but then his mind switched to preserving forensic evidence.

The man was dying, his mind shouted at him. Help him!

Patrick tried to ignore the feel of the blood on his hands as he pressed the wounds on Calum, trying to stem the blood flow. A major vein must've been cut, he thought as the blood seeped through his fingers.

The phone was by his legs, "Help me!" he shouted at the phone, but was unable to hear the reply.

At the sound of the footsteps he turned, expecting to see the high visibility coats of a paramedic or a police officer, but the fast moving boot of a hooded man caught his face.

He had no time to react and he fell backwards, rolling away. His instinct was to try and protect himself, and he recalled his training and kicked out at the man. The attacker was above him and Patrick saw the blood covered knife in his hand.

The man kicked out again and leaned down to slash at Patrick. Patrick kicked out himself, catching the man on his knee, and then pulled the attacker close to him, but the knife came dangerously close to his face. With a sharp punch to his bicep, the man dropped the knife.

Patrick tried to punch the man, to try and hurt him in any way, but he was faster than Patrick. His hands and elbows landed hard on Patrick's body and he gasped for air.

He was desperate to get the man off him and with the attackers hands around his neck, Patrick gripped hard to free himself, scratching at the arms and gloved hands. The attacker landed heavily on him and he slammed Patrick's head into the hard floor, dazing him.

Patrick loosened his grip and slumped down onto the floor and with his brain trying to restart his body, his weary eyes watched as the man picked his knife up again, knelt next to Calum, and slowly pushed the blade into his chest, piercing his heart.

Patrick was horrified as he witnessed the murder and he tried to move as the attacker calmly stood up and dropped a piece of paper on the floor. *GLUTTONY.*

CHAPTER 22

Daniel sat on the sofa, and looked through the notes he had scattered around. Following his sudden departure from the newspaper, he had managed to gather some of his files and notes from his desk. But for the majority of it, he had to try and recall from memory and write again.

When he planned an article, he always wrote ideas down, things that occurred to him for possible avenues of investigation. He would try to allow his mind to work the problem, mull it over and then let his reasoned logical brain construct ideas, questions and scenarios.

He hadn't been to any of the other police press conferences for the other murders and had spent the past few hours searching the internet for footage of them. Some websites only carried edited versions of the briefings, a few minutes long, but he needed the full version to try and get as much information as possible.

He had been sitting there since Georgina had left, and as he sat back he thought about her again.

He couldn't believe what had happened between them. They had soon moved from the sofa to his bedroom where their clothes had been discarded and they had engaged in passionate sex.

It had felt right. It was the only way he could describe it.

It was comfortable, with no feeling of embarrassment or guilt. They both knew it was what they wanted, and as soon as the opportunity arrived to get it, they took it. He didn't know if Georgina felt the same way. He smiled to himself as he remembered that they didn't really talk much during or after. It was almost as if they were teenagers, giggling and playfully touching each other as the realisation of what they had done sank into them both.

But he felt he could see something deep within her eyes, that the actions she took, were something she had wanted for a while, and as she felt the warmth of the moment writhe through her for the second time, he could almost see the stress of the past days release from her sexy body.

Perhaps he was right in what he saw, he thought, or more likely, he saw what he wanted to see. As men so often do.

He checked his phone again for any messages from her, thinking it was a ridiculous thing to do as the phone was on vibrate and ring. If she had messaged, he would've known. But it was nearing midnight, and she would be in bed at home now. With Patrick.

Patrick.

Daniel had tried not to think about the betrayal he had committed against his brother. He knew what he had done was wrong. It would destroy him, Daniel thought. It wouldn't just break up their marriage, but it would also break their brotherly bond.

James had been right. He shouldn't have pursued her, he shouldn't have acted upon his urges. Whether Patrick and Georgina got a divorce or not, the fact would always remain that Daniel had betrayed his brother, and because of that, he would be the one annexed from the family, and would forever be on the outside. He couldn't remain in contact with either of them. There was no chance of he and Georgina making a life together away from Patrick, he was her children's father after all, he would always be in her life.

But wasn't Patrick bringing his marriage to an end anyway with his own actions?

With his own affair being discovered, their marriage could be over soon anyway. If it was and they did get a divorce, would it be accepted if Daniel and Georgina were to become a couple? Daniel wouldn't be to blame, Patrick would.

It wasn't unheard of for women to marry their husbands brother after a divorce, he thought. But granted, most of those people were usually seen on a trashy daytime chat show being berated by an arrogant roaming moderator.

He checked his phone again, still no message.

Daniel shook his head and tried to rid himself of the thoughts of Georgina, at least for a while, he promised. He had work to do.

With the video file now loaded on the computer, he started to play the full press conference footage from the police following the murder of the homeless man, Leo Banner.

He watched as the usual procession of police senior officers emerged from the wings like they were stepping onto the stage. They each took their seats and then they started with the usual introductions.

Already Daniel was finding his mind wandering back to Georgina, and the image of her kneeling over him, naked, and then leaning down to kiss him.

He must've closed his eyes for a second as he sat up quickly at the sudden sound of his phone ringing. He saw on the screen it was Georgina and he answered it. "Was just thinking of you." He said with a smile.

He listened to her for a second, ignoring the footage on his computer screen. "Okay," he said, all fun and banter gone from his demeanour. "Send the kids to your parents, and I'll meet you there."

*

The hospital had been billed as a 'Super-Hospital' in the press and by the Government. Costing in excess of £250million, it was a state of the art facility that combined the now closed down local hospital units into one site.

Daniel ignored the fancy architecture as he quickly dodged the couple ambling through the revolving door. He looked up at the departments board and headed towards the emergency department.

In the long white corridor, he saw Georgina ahead of him and he called out to her.

"What's happened?" he said once he caught up with her.

There was a moment of unease between them as they stood together. Given the carnal intimacy they had enjoyed together, they both felt uneasy. Perhaps what they did was wrong; perhaps it would ruin their relationship.

Daniel could sense the unease between them, and while he wanted to try and ease the discomfort for them both by giving her hug, but thought better of it.

He could tell she had been crying and despite his better judgement, he pulled her to him. There was a second of tension there, but then she relaxed and embraced him back. "What's happened?" he asked again.

She pulled away from him and continued walking. "I'm not sure." She said. "He's been attacked. Nobody can tell me what happened."

Together they walked towards the emergency department and at the double doors, she turned to Daniel. "Danny, about what happened -"

"I know." He interrupted her. "Let's not think about that at the moment, as hard as it is not to." He said.

She smiled at him and stepped up and kissed him on the lips. "You're an amazing man." She said.

They headed into the department and were met by a sea of police officers. Georgina stopped short at the sight of them all, but Daniel took her hand and walked them through the officers.

He knew why they were there. It happened every time a fellow police officer was injured on duty. The brotherly bond between the officer came to the forefront and they all banded together to try and do whatever they could to help. Most of them were excess to requirements, and they thought they were needed there rather than out on the streets trying to find the attacker.

Daniel could see that in an already busy department, the doctors and nurses weren't appreciative of the extra people getting in their way.

Daniel and Georgina found the nurses desk and asked for Patrick. They were directed to a room further down the corridor. As they approached, they saw the two armed guards standing at the door who looked them both up and down. Neither officer stood to the side to allow them into the room.

"This is DI King's wife." Daniel said.

"And you?" one of the officers asked.

"I'm his brother."

Still neither man let them enter. "Sorry, but the Chief Superintendent and others are in there. They'll be done in a minute."

Daniel was about to protest and point the ridiculous reasoning of stopping the man's wife go in to see him, but Georgina accepted the excuse and stepped away from the officers, Daniel following.

"Forensics are at the scene now." Detective Chief Superintendent Withers said. "The post mortem will be this afternoon."

Patrick lay in bed and watched as Michael Ferguson, the scenes of crime officer, took swab samples from underneath his fingernails and packaged them individually. He had already taken a series of photographs, documenting the injuries to his face, and as he finished off with the fingernail samples, he patted Patrick on the arm.

"Glad you're okay boss," he said. "We'll have to come back for more photos when the bruising comes out later."

Patrick nodded and adjusted himself on the bed.

"How long will it take to get something back off them?" Withers asked, nodding at the swab samples.

Ferguson thought for a moment. "A few days at least." He said. "If we can get them to the lab today, they might be able to fast track them. It will cost you though."

Withers nodded and turned to Helen Kolar who was sitting at the side of the bed. "Helen, can you get them off ASAP, I'll authorise the expense."

She nodded.

Ferguson packed up his case and left the officers in the room, and as the door closed Withers turned to Patrick. "You understand Patrick that you will need to be interviewed later and give a statement, and until you're recuperated you will be taken off duty."

"I shouldn't be off too long." Patrick said.

"You've a dislocated thumb, and fractured wrist. And until that bruising on your face and body goes down, you're not to come to the station."

"But I can still work." He protested.

"You need to rest." Helen said, looking at him and catching his eye.

"Who will take over?" Patrick asked, looking at her and stroking her hand subtly. He winced as his chest tightened.

Withers looked at Helen Kolar. "I've spoken to Helen and she's agreed to act up for the foreseeable future."

Patrick nodded and smiled at her. It was a good opportunity for her, he thought, a chance to make a name for herself, and with the future he had planned for them both, a good way to get them both settled.

"There is one thing though," Assistant Chief Constable Clarkson said. "What were you doing there? How did Calum Book fit into our investigation?"

Patrick had known this question was coming. He had tried to think of an excuse, a reason for being there. Was it to do with the investigation? He couldn't lie, he would soon be found out.

"It was personal." He said finally.

"Personal?" Clarkson asked. "How?"

"I'd rather not say." Patrick added.

Withers knew the man had been through a near fatal attack, but he still needed answers. He had heard of Calum Book before, and knew about the scandals that followed the man around. He was also aware of the connection between Book and Daniel King.

Clarkson was about to ask again when Withers spoke up. "We can sort out all of this later," he said, locking eyes with Patrick, trying to mentally pass to him that he knew about the family connection. "But as you're no longer the lead investigator, I have to ask if you have any documentation at home relating to it."

Patrick looked at his superior, and his mind flashed with images of the documents at home. They were confidential documents and should be at the police station, he wasn't allowed to take them home. But he did anyway, most senior officers did.

He had found that reading through them away from the incident room added clarity to his thoughts. But he could see the trouble that was heading towards him now if he admitted to it.

"Call it an amnesty." Withers said, smiling sickly and false. "We just need to know if you have anything at home."

Patrick quickly ran through the permutations and hidden meaning behind the statement. An amnesty? A chance to admit to things without fear of prosecution? Why should he fear anything? Unless there was something he didn't know about.

What could it be? He asked himself. And what was that look Withers had given him when asking about him being there at Book's apartment.

Did Withers know about Daniel and Calum Book's connection? Could that be it? Was Patrick actually under suspicion for attacking Book?

"No," he said finally. "Nothing's at home."

Withers appeared to be satisfied with his answer, but his eyes shot him a quick look, one that told Patrick he thought he was lying. "We'll leave you to rest." He said, shaking Patricks hand and heading to the door.

As she stood, Patrick reached for Helen's hand, and their fingers brushed against each other. He felt the softness of her skin, the warmth of her hand, but she didn't squeeze his hand back as she followed her superiors out.

He watched her leave and then saw Georgina enter the room, followed by Daniel.

"What's he doing here?" he asked.

"Patrick!" Georgina snapped.

"Good to see you're back to your normal charming self." Daniel said.

Georgina shot him a look, as if to tell them both to grow up.

"I'll leave." Daniel said. "Glad you're OK."

Patrick mumbled a thanks, but there was no real effort in it as Daniel reached the door and headed back into the corridor. "I'll call you later, to check on him." Daniel said, his eyes lingering on Georgina for a second.

"You could've been nicer." Georgina said to Patrick, trying to regain her composure.

He scoffed at her. "Please. It's because of him I'm here."

"How can you think that?"

"It's complicated." He replied. "But-"

"What?" she asked. "He's done nothing to you, you've brought this on yourself."

Patrick wasn't in the mood for an argument and let the comment pass. But as they fell into a lingering silence, he began to think about what his superiors had been saying. He thought for a moment, "I think some shit is about to head my way."

He quickly explained to her that he had some documents at home.

"Just hand them back." She said.

He shook his head. "I can't." he said. "They say now that nothing will happen, but I think the knives are out for me, and I need to give them as little ammunition as possible. If those documents are found at home, in my office, then I'll be slung before professional standards."

There was a silence between them, and they both knew they were thinking about his admission of an affair. He didn't know what to say to her, he didn't really want to talk about it, but he knew there must come a time when they should.

Georgina didn't look at her husband, but studied her hands and then spotted the empty jug of water. "I'll get some iced water." She said.

As she headed down the corridor she felt the relief of leaving the room. She hadn't expected to feel that way around her husband, but perhaps the knowledge of the affair had hit her deeper than she realised.

Or maybe it was her own guilt?

As she thought about Daniel once more, she pulled her phone from her pocket and dialled his number. She didn't know why she should be helping Patrick, why she was going to assist in essentially a crime. Perhaps it was the loyalty of being married, and as much as she hated Patrick, she didn't want to see his career collapse for having confidential documents at home.

With anxious anticipation she felt her heart beat faster as he answered the phone. "Danny," she said, "I need you to do me a favour. I need you to find something in Patricks office at home."

PART FIVE

ENVY

CHAPTER 23

The days had been too long for him.

Daniel had split his time focusing on the pages of confidential information he had taken from Patrick's home office, and thinking about Georgina.

Following her phone call as he left the hospital, she had begged him to go over to her house and collect the files from his desk. He had at first asked if she was joking, and wanted to know why he should help him. But she had soon persuaded him to help, saying he was never the type of person to knowing let somebody down.

He had reluctantly agreed and headed over.

Daniel had been expecting to find only one or two folders, but as he entered the office he saw nearly half a box full of photos, documents, statements and notes. Georgina had been right, he thought. If Patrick's superiors ever found this information in his house, he would lose his job. But what would happen if the police found it in Daniel's flat?

He knew he shouldn't be reading the files, they were confidential and if he was found to be in possession of them, he would be prosecuted and jailed. He had heard prison food wasn't too bad, he thought as he smiled to himself.

But his journalistic instincts were too strong to resist.

He couldn't believe the information he was reading. The photos were graphic, images of the crime scenes, the bodies, the wounds and blood. The post mortem photos were worse, and Daniel had to close the album.

He couldn't remember how much sleep he had over the last few days, but as he turned the pages and started another statement, he ignored the tiredness. The information he had at his disposal could easily be constructed into the greatest media story ever, but he also knew he had to be careful.

Using too much first-hand information could bring to much suspicion on himself, and therefore a lengthy prison sentence. He needed to find a delicate balance between creativity and plagiarism.

His own notes were extensive and Daniel copied another snippet of information.

He had come to realise that there were more witnesses to the murders than the police had released to the press. Some of the statements were forthcoming in the information passed, but others were short and not so sweet. The side notes made by the officers showed their frustrations with editorials of *'Useless witness'* and *'Needs further questioning'.*

He checked his watch and saw the date on the corner of the dial change to 24th December. Christmas Eve.

He had been contacted by James and had been persuaded once more to join him at Patrick's and Georgina's house for Christmas lunch. It would be the first time they would've been together for an extended period of time and he hoped it wouldn't descend into an argument and fight.

But it was for the kids, he thought. He had promised Charlie he would be there for his first mass as an altar server and as much as he had issues with Patrick, he would try his best to be there.

He looked at his notes and rubbed his tired eyes. He needed sleep and made a mental note to try and track down one of the witnesses in the morning. There was something not quite sitting comfortably with him, and he wanted clarification.

Moving away from his desk, he checked his mobile phone. There was still no message from Georgina.

She turned over in bed and saw the red glow of the digital clock stare back at her. Georgina hadn't slept well, as she hadn't for the past few days. Her mind had been awash with frantic thoughts, of Patrick, of Daniel, her family, and her future.

She had long held onto the belief that her marriage was strong enough to withstand anything, and with the recovery of her senses following Patrick's previous affair, she thought things were safe. She had never thought or believed he would risk their marriage and family again, considering how close they had come to splitting before.

216

But she was now in turmoil herself as she thought about Daniel. He had been in her life longer than Patrick, but a twist of their paths led them apart, and took her to Patrick's side.

She had to admit that she had always had feelings for Daniel, but she had long believed them to be those of a sibling. However, following their intimate encounter, feeling his body against hers and sensing the passion he had for her, she knew her feelings were developing, or had already long ago developed into something more.

Since the attack on Patrick, she had played the role of doting wife and had looked after him. Things had been almost normal, with Patrick being at home they had spent time as a family. As the days ticked by and got closer to Christmas, the excitement of the children was starting to rub off on them both, and she was starting to look forward to festive celebrations.

Patrick had been released from the hospital two days after the attack, and while he struggled with the smallest things, buttoning his shirt and holding a pen, he was adjusting to his limitations.

He had asked about the files in his office as she drove him home from the hospital. She stayed quiet for a moment, not wanting to tell him Daniel had taken them, so she lied. "One of your team came round yesterday," she had said, "I gave them to him." She didn't expand on it anymore and the rest of the journey was in silence.

Perhaps he knew she was lying, she thought, and that Daniel did have the files, but he didn't say anything.

She could see the positive difference that time away from his work was having on his behaviour and on their home life, but then she saw his mobile phone flashing.

She didn't know why she picked it up, but she saw it was a message from Helen Kolar, and despite her strongest will, she opened the message and read the message thread that had been sent over the past days and nights.

There was no way of describing how her heart jumped into spasm and she almost collapsed to her knees as she read their conversation and declared that they missed each other. She scrolled through further and saw Patrick was making references to the future, and at one point a holiday together. It was then she stopped reading. She could no longer stomach the betrayal he had brought on her yet again.

Later that evening, once the children had gone to bed, Patrick had asked where his phone was, and as she calmly passed it to him, she said "You may want to reply to your lover, I'm sure she's getting anxious."

Patrick was about to reply, but Georgina simply turned to walk out of the room but he grabbed her arm. She turned to him calmly and looked him in the eyes. "Take your hands off me, or you'll never get access to the children again." He released her. "You promised you'd never lie to me again," she continued, her voice controlled and measured, "but how wrong you were."

She didn't say any more as she left the living room and headed to bed.

She had lay in bed listening to the sounds of the house, of Patrick walking around downstairs, all through the sobs of her own crying. She listened as Patrick came upstairs, and wondered what she would do when he entered the bedroom, but he never did. She heard the spare bedroom door open and close, and the tears ran down her face again.

There was tension between them over breakfast, there was no denying it. Patrick may have slept well, she thought, but she could almost taste the bitterness that had grown between them.

She knew Charlie and Clarissa could sense it too. It was Christmas Eve and instead of being excited and bouncing around, they were subdued as if they were too nervous to speak.

"I'm heading into work later." Patrick said.

"Okay." Georgina replied simply. She really wasn't in the mood to talk or converse with him and she kept her answers short and to the point.

"I need to be brought up to speed on things before I start back next week." He explained.

"I said okay." She replied.

"I don't know how long I'll be."

Georgina shot him a look, "Does that matter? You come and go as you please."

"Georgie –"

"Don't –" she snapped. "Just do what the hell you want and we'll see you whenever you decide you've had your fill there."

"It's not like that!" Patrick protested.

She shrugged, "Whatever it is, I'm sure you'll make an excuse." She stood and headed to the stairs, "Sort them out, I'm going for a bath."

Patrick watched his wife leave the kitchen and he looked over and saw the confused faces of his children.

"Why's mummy angry?" Clarissa asked.

Patrick felt his heart almost break as his daughter asked the honest question. There really was no way of hiding the fractures in their marriage from them. "Daddy did something wrong." He said. "He's sorry, but mummy is still angry."

"Will Santa still come?" Charlie asked meekly.

Patrick smiled at them and crouched beside them, hugging them. "Of course he will. You've done nothing wrong. He'll always come for you."

CHAPTER 24

"To see the life ebb from the dying face of a man is one of the most gratifying images to witness. Gluttony is an evil sin. He embellished himself in materialistic items with no care in the world. He had never once faced a day of work, a day of suffering, a day of pain or a day of heartbreak. Everything he ever wanted, he was given, and everything he ever dreamed of he was granted. He had never lived with disappointment, and he had never seen suffering – until he saw his own demise."

James sat in the confessional and listened to the man speak. He hadn't said anything since the man had knelt down and he listened to the confession of the killer.

"It was as if there was a moment of clarity in his eyes." He said. *"A moment when he realised his life had been wasted. There was desperation and pleading there, he wanted to be saved, he wanted somebody to help him. But he had lived a life where everybody had bowed down to him and helped him in everything, he had never worked*

for anything in his life, and in his death, nobody could help him again."

"And the other man you attacked?" James asked. He had heard from Daniel that Patrick had been attacked, and he thanked God he was safe, although bruised and beaten. He could feel the anger within him build as the man casually confessed his sins, and there was part of him that hated the man, hated and detested the man who so calmly attacked his brother.

"Ah yes," the man said, almost smiling. *"He was an unexpected visitor, and unexpected and exciting twist. He suffered, but he was not part of my overall objective. He was not part of the Lord's plan. He suffered, he saw death, but perhaps now he will be wiser. Perhaps now he will see the world with more clarity than before. He will see the world through others eyes, rather than his own narrow field of view. Your brother was lucky."*

James felt himself go rigid at the direct mention of his brother. *Could it be right? Could this man, this killer, know of James' family?* If he did, were the rest of his family safe? Was Daniel, Georgina, Charlie and Clarissa?

He could no longer control his anger. "How do you know about my family? How?"

Silence.

"You shall not be absolved from your sins until you answer me!"

James heard the steady breathing, *"I shall Fr. King. You are too loyal to your oath not to absolve me. I accept your forgiveness."*

There was a movement behind the curtain and it took James a second before he realised the man had left the booth. Quickly he moved from his chair and pulled the curtain back.

The church was quietly active with helpers preparing for the celebrations later that evening, and James looked around himself for any sign of the man. At the far corner he saw the doors closing and at a run he raced over to the door, dodging the cleaners who were vacuuming the carpet. He didn't apologise as he skipped over the machine being dragged behind her and he burst through the doors into the foyer.

He caught sight of the heavy oak door closing and he raced to it pushing it open and emerging into the cold winter morning.

On the lawn was the large Christmas tree, illuminated by thousands of lights, and the few parked cars on the roadside sat silently. James looked around himself, but couldn't see any sign of the man.

With the large playing fields opposite the church, dotted with trees, and the road next to the church leading to a maze of junctions there were a thousand places for the man to hide.

He was gone.

James silently cursed as he frustratingly banged his fist against the wrought iron gate, rattling it.

How could he let the man escape again? He thought. *How?*

There was nothing he could do, he knew. He couldn't break his promise and vow, he couldn't confide in anyone but God himself. He turned back to the church and entered, saying a prayer and asking for forgiveness himself for cursing.

*

He had slept too well, and despite knowing his body and mind, he obviously needed it and was starting to feel the repercussions now.

His body was still tight from sleeping at an awkward angle on the sofa. He should've gone to bed when he had the momentum to walk, but he collapsed where he could and the sofa was the first thing he landed on.

Daniel stretched his muscles as he walked across the car park and stepped out onto the street.

He was in a former industrial area of the city, once alive with activity of the factories, it was now a shell of its former self. The once architecturally impressive buildings were now shells, empty and home to handfuls of pigeons, birds and vagabonds.

The machinery had long ago stopped working and been ripped out. The lights and wiring had been pilfered by thieves eager to make easy money at the high prices of copper on the open market.

Daniel headed down the road and crossed over towards the Cross Keys Nightclub. He had the scene photos from the first murder in a folder in his hand as he headed towards the back of the Club. He tried to orientate them so he could sense how the crime looked in those first hours.

He looked up and down the alleyway, spotting the location where the couple were stabbed, now indicated by a few sagging flowers and a wet teddy bear. There was no other indication that two people had died there and as he stepped along the path, he noticed he made a conscious effort to step around their last resting place.

The alleyway was like any other. Large rubbish bins lined the walls, rusting black metal stairs and fire escapes snaked down the side of the buildings. Boxes of empty bottles and bags of filth were strewn everywhere. Daniel could've also sworn he heard the scurrying of rats all around him. He couldn't see any CCTV cameras on the wall, and according to the reports of the officers attending, the only ones available were inside the Club and at the entrance.

He walked towards the front of the club, and saw the cameras looking down at him.

He didn't know what he expected to find. He always doubted the full capabilities of police officers, having heard stories of some of them missing the simplest of clues and evidence, or bypassing lines of enquiry because it seemed like too much hard work. But ignoring and not finding the CCTV from the nightclub would be a basic mistake for all persons involved.

Within the files he had studied back home, Daniel found a note in Patrick's handwriting saying that no decent images of the offender could be seen on the grainy footage.

There goes the CCTV, he thought.

In his shoulder bag Daniel carried a select few of the documents and turned to one of the pages and found the copy of the statement of one of the witnesses that was interviewed on the night. When he had read the documents, there were a few questions he thought should've been asked, avenues that should've been explored more than they actually were.

He checked the name at the top of the page, William "Billy" Chandler, and he had given his address as the Lion

Public House. Daniel looked across the road and saw the Lion pub and headed over to it.

Inside was dark, despite the afternoon light trying to penetrate the filtered windows. Shadows were cast across the wooden bar and aged barman. The pool table, stained from hundreds of drinks spilt on it over the years sat disused and tattered.

The small battered worn and torn stools were placed around the scarred tables, and the faux leather seats that lined the walls had seen an accumulative collection of a thousand backsides squashing the cushions.

On the wall was a large TV playing the traditional satellite sports station and a random football match of South American teams was playing.

Daniel walked in, knowing he was out of place, knowing he wasn't a local and knowing he would face aggression and resistance from the drinkers. He approached the bar, spying the drinks available and wondered when the last time the pipes on the beer pumps had been cleaned.

Perhaps something stronger would be safer, he thought.

"Double whiskey." He said, nodding to the optics behind the large bulbous barman.

The man reluctantly moved from his stool and ambled over to the bottle and poured two shots into a glass. Daniel was about to ask for ice, but thought better of it. Paying, Daniel took a sip, wincing at the shock of the alcohol against his senses.

"I'm trying to find William Chandler." He asked the barman.

The barman looked Daniel up and down, inspecting him, his untrusting eyes wavering over him. "You a cop?"

Daniel smiled, trying to ease the tension. "No. But I understand he knows something about those two kids who were stabbed a couple of weeks back?"

"What do you care about it?"

He shrugged, trying to be nonchalant. "I just want to ask a couple of questions myself."

"Why?"

Daniel could understand the resistance, and the refusal to speak to a police officer. In a place like this, officers of the law would be greeted with a broken bottle rather than a welcoming hand. "I'm an investigator for the family," he lied, "They think the police screwed up and I need to re-examine what the police did so I can throw it back in their face and embarrass them." He didn't want to tell the barman he was a reporter as he had learned over the years that reporters were often viewed with as much suspicion as police. "I just want to speak to him." He added

"Billy told the police he saw nothing."

Daniel took another sip of his drink and thought about the words. He frowned and mulled over the answer again. He turned to the barman who had resumed his position at the far end of the bar. "You *say* he saw nothing. What did he actually see?"

"You best finish your drink mate." The barman said.

Daniel stepped further along the bar. "Look, I'm not a copper, I just want to speak to Billy to find out what he saw. I want to get some details so I can embarrass them."

The barman stilled eyed Daniel with suspicion, but then finally nodded to a man sat in the corner. "It'll cost you a drink to speak to him."

"What does he drink?"

"Whiskey." Daniel ordered a double shot, but the barman shook his head, smiling. "Nah mate," he continued, "You need a bottle." He said, pulling a bottle of cheap whiskey from under the bar and placing it before Daniel.

He looked at the bottle, then at the drunk in the corner. It was the best lead he had, and the only way forward was to buy the bottle. Reluctantly he pulled his wallet out and paid.

With the bottle in his hand he walked towards the man and put it on the table. The man looked at the bottle then followed the hand and arm to the man standing over him.

"Hi there Billy," Daniel said. "I'd like a word if I may."

CHAPTER 25

Charlie was eager to get going. The Christmas Eve mass was due to start in an hour, and he wanted to get to the church early to help prepare things. He called for his mother again as he stood in the living room with Clarissa sitting watching TV.

Upstairs, Georgina heard Charlie call her and she shouted down she would be there in a minute. She held her phone to her ear and listened to the ringing tone as she tried to contact Patrick. Once more she heard the recorded message.

"Patrick, it's me." She said, trying to keep her voice calm. "We're about to head over to the Church. Charlie is asking for you, so I hope you'll be there for him."

She hung up and sat quietly for a moment.

He had headed back to the office earlier in the day, and they hadn't spoken when he left. She really didn't know if he was going to show up at the church or not. She had found herself dreading spending time with him, but despite her burning and growing hatred towards her husband, she hoped he would be there for the good of Charlie.

Charlie had asked all day if daddy would be coming, and she had at first lied saying she was sure he would come. But as the day drew on, she wasn't sure if he would be coming. She knew that children were resilient and would hide their disappointment from their parents, and it broke her heart to see the drop in Charlie's shoulders as he realised his father wouldn't be there.

She wiped a tear from her face and headed downstairs, grabbing her car keys. "Come on then." She said cheerfully, "let's get you there to make your debut."

She could only smile as Charlie sat in the back of the car and directed Georgina towards the church. He was so excited about being there, he was telling her to take short-cuts and to jump red lights. He was sitting behind her, and she could feel his foot pressing into her back as he pressed the imaginary accelerator.

Finally, they arrived at the church and before she had gathered her bag, Charlie was out of the car and running up the steps.

Inside was beautiful, she thought. The large tree on the altar twinkled with thousands of lights. The nativity scene was set up in the side chapel and between the stone columns leading down the length of the church, holly and ivy was hanging between them.

Charlie was heading towards the front of the church when she saw Fr. William.. He welcomed them with open arms.

"Merry Christmas." William said.

"Merry Christmas Fr William." Charlie said.

"Where's your husband? Will he be joining us?" William asked.

Georgina looked away, almost embarrassed. "He's back at the office. I have no idea if he's coming."

"A demanding role your husband has," William said, "I'm sure God will forgive him this once."

Fair play if God will, Georgina thought, *nobody else would.*

"Well," William said, turning to Charlie. "Are you ready?"

"Yes!" he said, almost jumping on the spot.

"Bad news though," William continued. "I've just been informed that your uncle James has been called to the Hospice. There's a patient there he needs to see. The family are quite upset. But don't worry, he has entrusted your debut performance to myself."

Charlie visibly looked deflated at not having his uncle or father there, Georgina thought. "He may be back in time," she said, "Go with Fr. William and get things ready."

Charlie gave a little smile and nodded.

Patrick saw her number flashing on his phone and switched it off. He wasn't in the mood to talk to his wife. He was sitting in what used to be his old office, watching Helen Kolar on the phone as she chased up an officer for an answer.

He was once more impressed by her professionalism and dedication to her job. With it being Christmas Eve, most senior officers in her position would've left early and headed home, leaving the staff to stay and continue the hard graft. Patrick gave a small smile, as he knew he was one of those who make a run for the door at the first opportunity.

But there she was, still working hard as the clock ticked closer to 7pm. She was really an inspiration to all, he thought. The police force could be a better place if there were more officers as dedicated and ambitious as she was.

And he would be with her.

When she hung up the phone they smiled at each other.

"You look very comfortable behind that desk." Patrick said.

"It feels comfortable." She said. "Although I have put a request in for a bigger chair."

Patrick laughed. "Is everything okay?"

"Fine." She said. "Good intelligence is coming in. The public are contacting us, I guess those appeals on the evening news helped."

"And the Forensics?"

Helen dropped the smile, Patrick noted, but only slightly. "You mean from your ordeal?"

Patrick shrugged. "Maybe."

Helen seemed to think for a second, whether she should share the information with him. Reluctantly she opened a folder. "The results are back."

Patrick stood and walked around the desk, looking out into the main office and seeing it was empty. "They all gone?"

"I let them go." She said. "I'm on cover tonight."

"So we're alone?"

Helen smiled and pointed at the file. "You wanted this?"

"To begin with." He said, giving her a wink of the eye.

He leaned over and started to read the report of the results on the nail swabs taken when he had been in hospital. As he read, he could smell Helen's perfume gently surround him, and the memories of them being together started to build up within him.

He re-focused his mind and read the report again, and when he reached the end he was stuck for words. "Inconclusive?"

Helen nodded. "I checked as soon as I read it. There was what they called a mixed profile, and it was bouncing back as your partial DNA, which given the swab was from under your nails, was sort of expected."

"So there're no new leads?"

Helen looked at him. "You're not officially on this case."

Patrick looked her in the eye. "Come on – you can tell me."

"How about I tell you afterwards?"

He looked at her. "After what?"

"After you kiss me." She said, leaning over and kissing him on the lips.

The *quick chat* had turned into an afternoon drinking session. Daniel emerged from The Lion pub feeling worse than when he entered. His mind was spinning as he tried to steady himself from the effects of the alcohol he had consumed.

Billy Chandler was an experienced drinker, and he could easily hold his own in any drinking challenge. The bottle of whiskey was nearly empty by the time Daniel stumbled out, and despite feeling the pain throb in his mind, he knew it was worth it.

Billy had been reluctant to talk at first, but he soon loosened up and started talking about the night of the first murders. He had described standing outside the Lion, smoking. He watched as a car, a hatchback, crawled past the club and then past the alleyway.

He hadn't really paid much attention to it until he saw it drive past a third time and pull into a side road. He had tried his hardest to remember the registration number.

Daniel had tried to get it from him, but all he got was *"red car, small, ends in RCC"*. It was better than nothing, Daniel thought.

Billy had then gone on to describe the man driving it, and Daniel scribbled down the description. It was nothing special. There were no detailed descriptions or significant items he could remember, but Billy had said he had seen the man before, maybe at the homeless hostel three streets over.

Daniel had thought that was a possibility, as the other murder victim was a homeless man. *But could the killer be a homeless person? With a car?* He doubted it.

As the conversation ebbed and weaved through Billy's tattered and drink fragmented memory, Daniel knew he had got as much as he was going to get from him and left Billy to continue the bottle on his own.

Daniel was regretting the final drink as he headed back towards his car. He knew he wasn't fit to drive home, but he needed the bag from the back of the car if he was to try and find a hotel for the night.

The car park was quiet and most of the other cars had gone. The last minute Christmas present buying finally completed. He dug into his pocket and found his keys and unlocked his car. Standing back up he thought he saw something behind him, and turning, the dark shadowed face of a hooded man rushed forward and punched him in the chest.

"Are you looking for me?" the man said.

Daniel reached out to the man, but then felt the pain shoot through his body. He looked down and saw the edge of the silver blade piercing his chest.

Fr. William was presiding over the mass, and as he recited the Eucharist prayer, Charlie was helping the more experienced altar boy prepare Communion.

Georgina sat and watched him, smiling as he perfectly followed the instructions and stood solemnly at the side, waiting for the priest to turn to them.

Their kissing was frantic, passionate, and as he held her against the wall, Patrick was eager to make love to Helen. She lifted her skirt up and moved his hands down, feeling her body, and moved himself between her legs.

Helen was just as eager and she reached down and unbuckled his trousers.

They paused as she moved onto the desk and Patrick moved between her legs, penetrating into her body.

Daniel looked at the blood on his hands and fell on his knees. His mind was numb as the pain pulsated through his body. He looked up at the man who was standing over him and, as the knife came swinging down once more, he tried to protect himself, but the slash of the blade against his hands caused him to fall back.

The congregation was quietly walking towards the altar, patiently taking it in turns for communion and wine; the Body and Blood of Christ.

Georgina stood in line and as she stepped forward she smiled at Charlie, who tried not to smile back, as he stood next to Fr. William. He held a plate underneath her mouth as she accepted the Holy Sacrament.

"Amen." She said quietly, before smiling at Charlie again.

The desk was moving as Patrick pushed deeper and harder into Helen. She was moaning with satisfaction as each thrust brought her closer to orgasm.

Patrick was releasing the tension of the past few weeks and he held her legs tight as he pushed again and again. He was focused on making love to her and didn't care how much noise was coming from the office.

Daniel was on his front, lying between two cars. He still had strength to move and began to slowly crawl away from his attacker. He could hear another car engine somewhere, and thought if only he could make himself heard or seen, he might be saved.

He reached out waving his bloodied hand, just as the attacker grabbed him again and pulled him back in between the cars.

Daniel tried to grip the concrete to stop himself, the tips of his fingers scratching along the surface. His nails ripped and tore as he scrambled for purchase on anything that could stop him moving.

With communion finished, Charlie helped tidy away the silver plates and chalices with the other server. The choir were singing traditional hymns and they were reciting *O' Holy Night* as he finished his tasks and sat back down on the pews to the rear of altar.

He looked down at the congregation and saw his mother sitting and watching him, but he couldn't see his father or uncle anywhere.

The orgasm hit him hard and his body tensed up and he convulsed as he ejaculated. Helen lay back and allowed him to continue, far from satisfied herself, but she was glad he was.

They parted ways and Patrick sat back on the chair as Helen sat up and buttoned her blouse.

"Never done that on the bosses desk before." He said smiling broadly at her.

Daniel was face down and there was nothing he could do as he felt the blade pierce his back. He coughed and spluttered blood as his life was fading from him. He saw the shoes of the man step over him, and calmly walk away into the distance of the car park.

He watched as the man dropped a piece of paper behind him, and Daniel tried to focus on the word written on it: *ENVY.*

PART SIX

PRIDE & WRATH

CHAPTER 26

It was cold. Colder than usual, even for winter.

The New Year excitement and cheer had long since been forgotten. Subdued and ignored by Patrick as he made plans for his brother's funeral.

He sat in the limousine following the hearse carrying Daniel, and he looked out of the window as his mind recounted the previous two weeks.

He remembered how he had learned of the attack, hearing Helen's phone ring and the control room telling her there was another body. He had attended the scene with her and, entering the car park, he was stopped from getting further, other than the outer cordon. Helen had gone in and came back to the line where Patrick was shouting that as an Inspector, he should be allowed in. The uniformed officer said he was following the instructions of the Chief

Superintendent, and Helen interrupted them, telling Patrick the victim was Daniel.

He refused to believe her and pushed past the officer and Helen, telling them both that they either arrest him or let him by. Helen let him by, but warned him not to approach the body.

He shouldn't have seen him. He knew that now.

He had fallen to his knees as he saw his younger brother lying dead, the dark and crimson blood like a still pool ebbing its way from the body. His cries echoed around the car park, and officers were motioned to take Patrick away.

He refused to go home and waited in the car outside the cordon as he watched the Forensic teams arrive. He saw Michael Ferguson pull on his white suit and Patrick climbed out of the car and headed to him.

Ferguson saw him coming. He already knew it was his brother in the car park and he had no idea what to say to the DI.

"Boss." He said simply.

"Fergie," Patrick said, "do a good job on this one will you?"

"I always do." He replied. "But I understand."

Patrick knew he would be professional about his job, but he was also aware of the macabre sense of humour that bounces around at these type of scenes. He couldn't outright tell them how to behave and what to say, but he at least wanted them to be aware, more than usual, of the personal side of the murder. Hopefully, he thought, that would be enough to rein in the loose talk over his brothers body.

As he headed back to the car he saw Superintendent Withers. "I'm sorry for your loss." He said.

Patrick accepted the comment, but his mind totally wasn't working properly. So much had happened, so much was about to happen. He looked at his superior and realised he was still talking. "I don't know how much you've been told so far, but at the moment it looks like the same offender as the others. They found a note beside the body. It read 'Envy'."

"The deadly sins." Patrick said quietly. "It follows the others."

Withers looked at him, almost trying to choose his words. "We're not too sure." He said. "It looks as though he was robbed too. His wrist shows abrasions where his watch was, and his bag has been rummaged through. Obviously we don't know what's been taken."

Patrick thought for a moment. A robbery? That was a different M.O. to the other murders. "His watch was stolen? That's something we never looked at with the others. Perhaps other items were stolen from the other victims. If we look -"

"Patrick, you realise you can't continue on this case." Withers interrupted. "You're too close to it. It's a conflict of interests."

"What?! But I can help." Patrick said. "My team needs me to lead them on this. They need to check these things. You can't take me off it."

How could they do this to him? He was the officer in charge of the case and he had the best overall view of the investigation. Without him, they wouldn't be able to keep track of all of the evidence coming in. He was the keystone that held the team together.

Withers tried to guide Patrick away from earshot of the other officers. "You know you can't continue on this."

"I can do both." He replied quickly

"Patrick," Withers said, trying to calm him down. "You can't. You've lost your brother and you can't be in charge of the investigation."

"Then who will be?" Patrick snapped.

"Helen Kolar is taking formal control of the incident room." Withers said. "She was already running it following your attack so she's up to speed on everything, and her application for the role of Detective Inspector was confirmed today."

Patrick turned away from Withers. He couldn't be taken off the case, *he* needed to be the one to investigate Daniel's murder. Nobody else. "But I could -"

"Go home Chief Inspector King." Withers said formally. "Go home, and we'll keep you informed."

He turned from Patrick and he was left alone. Patrick leaned against the car and suddenly the strength in his knees fell away. He collapsed onto the concrete and held his head. Tears were streaming down his face and he looked through the blur of emotion and saw the activity of the officers as the Forensic teams headed into the scene and the television crews arrived. The officers held them back.

He saw the CID officers, his officers, talking amongst themselves and casting looks over to him. Some appeared to acknowledge him, giving consoling nods, others just looked and then turned away as he caught their eye. He watched Helen as she talked to them all, giving them instructions and tasks to do, lines of enquiries to follow, and he saw her as she walked gracefully and with the authority of being in charge as she talked to Withers.

They conversed for a couple of seconds and Patrick watched them,. He saw the gentle touch of hands of the two of them as they parted and the look Withers gave her as she left. The same look Patrick had given her every time he had seen her leave a room.

A look of wanting and desire.

The body had been released from the coroners within a week, and just after New Year, when the population were still nursing hangovers, Patrick and James had attended the funeral directors.

They were compassionate and understanding for their needs. James wished to conduct the ceremony himself, and Patrick give the eulogy. They both agreed that while a church funeral and mass would be a greater send off for Daniel, he would've objected to it, given his rejection of the church in his life. Therefore a local crematorium was selected and the date of the funeral was set.

Beside him in the limousine, Georgina was staring blankly out of the window at the line of trees that led their way to the crematorium. He wanted to reach out and hold her hand, give her some reassurance, but they hadn't been talking much since Christmas.

It was past midnight when he had arrived home on Christmas Eve. Georgina was still awake, pushing presents under the tree when he walked into the living room. She didn't acknowledge he was there and walked past him into the kitchen.

"George." He said quietly. "Something's happened."

She turned to him, finishing her glass of wine. "I know." She said. "I can smell her on you."

Patrick hung his head in shame and tried to gather his thoughts. It wasn't the time to have an argument or try to defend his actions. "Daniel's dead." He said quickly.

Georgina looked at him, "What?"

"He was attacked in a car park in town." Patrick said stepping towards her. "He was stabbed." He added, the emotion cracking in his voice.

Georgina reached out to him and hugged him as Patrick broke down and cried.

The rest of Christmas had been subdued. They had to tell Charlie and Clarissa about their uncle, but they decided to tell them after the excitement of unwrapping presents and the Christmas lunch had died down. Patrick had thanked Georgina's parents for joining them, to ease the burden of trying to keep the children occupied and also deal with the emotional turmoil inside.

"Where were you when Danny was killed?" Georgina asked as they stood in the kitchen while the kids watched another Christmas special TV programme.

Patrick couldn't look at her, and he didn't answer.

"You're a bastard Patrick." She said. "I will stand beside you until after the funeral, but then I want you out of this house."

"George -"

"You were screwing another woman when your brother was being murdered. You were fucking another woman when your son wanted you to be there at church." She wiped a tear from her face. "Danny was right, you live in your own little world and we all have to dance to your tune. Well no more. You walked this line, now you live with the consequences. I want you out."

Patrick had tried to talk to her, to try and talk sense to her, but she didn't listen. As he looked at her in the limousine, he wanted to hold her hand, he wanted to feel comfort from her, to know she was there for him. But would she give it?

He thought not.

The procession arrived at the crematorium and those in the official cars stepped out into a light rain. Charlie and Clarissa were with their grandparents, and Patrick greeted cousins and family friends who had arrived.

As the coffin emerged, James led the congregation into the chapel, followed by Daniel's ex-wife Samantha and their daughter Louise.

The service was plain. Opening prayers were given, hymns were sung, with James keeping his composure as he stood over the coffin of his older brother.

Patrick was introduced to give the eulogy. "I think if Danny was here," he said, "he'd probably be amazed at the number of people. It's fair to say that he touched more people than we realised. Myself and James are grateful that you could be here today.

"We all have our memories of Danny. Some good, some – not so – shall we say. But one thing we can all agree on is his devoted loyalty to his friends, and family. He would always be there for us, no matter what. His self-less attitude to go the extra mile should be an inspiration to us all, a demonstration of the true nature of man, and a guiding example to Louise of how to act in this savage world.

"All families have their issues. Ours was no different. Me and Danny had a number of arguments over the years, about different things, from college, girls, sport and careers. But his defining characteristic was of a man who would support you no matter what. He would help whenever he could, even if it was detrimental to his own cause. He was selfless. Something we should all try to be."

Patrick paused and blinked away the tears that were forming in his eyes. He looked over at Georgina, hoping to see his supportive wife, but he was met with a steely gaze of a woman trying to keep her own emotions in order. "I remember Danny caught me smoking once," Patrick said, "when I was about 14. I'd taken a couple of fags from our father's pack and I snuck off to the river near our house to light them up. I don't know how he knew I was there, but I was just taking that first drag when his head appeared from behind a tree. *Dad will belt you if he catches you!* He said. I coughed and hacked and told him to – well I told him to go away in an impolite manner." A small ripple of gentle laughter filtered around the chapel. "But he stayed and sat there with a cheeky smile watching me suffer. In the end he took the cigarette off me and smoked it himself. Not a single cough. He finished that thing off like a pro."

Patrick smiled to himself at the memory. "But that was him. He would chastise you on one hand, but then his own willingness to put himself at risk of our father's belt was on the other. If I was going to suffer, he was going to suffer too.

"I could talk about his career, his dreams, his aspirations and his loves. But, he was so many things to so many people. We all have our memories of him, that we should share and cherish. But I will say this. He was the reason I joined the police.

"He spoke passionately about it. He read books, watched TV shows, he found out everything he could about it, and then he would tell me and James all about it and how he would change the world, how he would make it better." Patrick bowed his head as he fought back the tears. "He would've been a hell of a good copper. He was one of the smartest people I knew, and I miss him dearly, and I love him. He's my brother, he will always be my brother, always be a father, a husband, an uncle, and he will always be our friend."

He stepped away from the podium and sat back down, wiping his face as the tears rolled down his cheek. James too was wiping his face as he blessed the coffin and the curtains slowly blocked it from view.

"Good bye, and God bless you."

CHAPTER 27

Despite the number of people at the wake, there was muted conversation all around. Patrick and Georgina's house was filled with people, friends and family, some of whom they hadn't seen for a few months, and for some years.

It was good, Patrick thought, to have so many people around as it took his mind off the past few hours. He didn't realise how stressed he had been, and now knowing that the funeral was over, he was starting to think more clearly.

On the stairs he saw the back of James sitting with Clarissa and Charlie, he stopped short and watched them.

"So -" Charlie said. "Uncle Danny is in heaven?"

"Yes he is." James replied. "I believe he is."

"Will God let him in?"

"He lets everyone in." James replied.

"Even the bad people?"

James thought for a second and Patrick smiled as he saw his brother struggle with the simplest theological question of a child. "He lets them in on the provision that they promise to behave." James answered.

Good answer, Patrick thought.

"Will Uncle Danny visit us?" Clarissa asked.

"No, no he won't." James said honestly. "But he won't have to. You know why? Because he'll always be here in our hearts, and always here in our heads, in our memories. Those times he played football with us, or built Lego. We all had fun times with him didn't we? We should share those stories and let others experience the time that we had with him. That's how his memory will live on."

Charlie and Clarissa seemed satisfied with the answers and they hugged their uncle. "Now," James said, "Louise is here somewhere, and I think she's very upset. Could you find her and play with her? Perhaps show her your new toys?"

"I can show her my new book." Clarissa said.

"And I can show her my new game, Master Pilot 3." Charlie said as they both jumped off the step and went to find Louise.

Patrick stepped forward. "Good handling of the *bad people* question."

"Thanks. It just came to me. I'll have to remember that one." James said.

"Drink?"

"Good god, yes please."

They both grabbed a glass of wine each and stood in the living room. At the far end Patrick could see Georgina talking to Samantha and her mother. He watched as she talked and she caught him looking at her. Her stare was cold and icy and she looked away.

"How are things with her?" James asked.

"Not good." Patrick said, swirling his drink around the glass. "She asked me to move out."

"When?"

"Tonight."

"I mean when did she tell you she wanted you out?"

Patrick downed his drink. "After the Queens Speech at Christmas."

"She'll change her mind." James said. "She's in shock."

Patrick shook his head. "No, this time she's thinking perfectly straight. She wants me out and I'll go. It'll be for the best."

"You can't leave." James said. "The kids have just lost their uncle, they can't lose you too."

"If I stay," Patrick replied, "they'll be exposed to arguing and fighting. How will that effect them? If I go peacefully, it will at least still keep the opportunity of reconciliation open. You're right, she's in shock, she needs time to come to terms with it all. If space is what she needs, then that's what she'll get."

"Where will you go?"

"I have somewhere I can stay." Patrick said, thinking of the large bed in Helen's house.

James looked at him, and saw the flicker of smile on his brothers face. He knew he was thinking of that other woman. "Well if that's not possible, come and stay at mine."

Patrick nodded. "Thanks. You're a good man."

"I learnt it off Danny."

The house reminded Patrick of the aftermath of his university house parties. Dirty glasses, plates, cutlery, empty bottles and uneaten food were scattered on any spare surface available. Patrick had a black bin bag and was throwing the rubbish out.

Georgina saw him cleaning up and took the bag from him. "I'll do it." She said.

"I can do it."

She faced him, her features showing no emotion. "You should be packing other bags." She said.

Patrick half threw his hands in the air. "Georgie, you can't be serious."

"Look at me Patrick," she said sternly. " Look at my face. I'm more serious about this than anything in my life. Get your bags, and get out. I'm sure your lady friend will be more than welcoming for you."

She continued to fill the rubbish bag with the debris of the wake, and Patrick walked slowly from the kitchen. He turned back to her. "I miss him so much." He said, "I don't want to lose you too."

"Well," she said, throwing the rubbish bag down. "Perhaps you should've thought about that before knobbing another woman."

Patrick was about to speak, but he thought better of it as he saw the raw anger in her eyes. He didn't want to infuriate her anymore. He knew he was in the wrong, and there was no way he could say anything to make her see sense. His sense. He wouldn't be able to make her see things from his point of view and he left the kitchen and walked upstairs.

Georgina tried to busy herself with the cleaning, but it was no good. She stopped and closed her eyes, gripping the counter top to steady herself, she closed her eyes to fight back the emotion.

She knew Patrick was hurting, she wasn't blind to his pain. But he was blind to the pain he had caused her. She was losing her husband because of his desires of another woman, and she had lost a man who had been one of her oldest friends and had become her own lover. Perhaps that night was only ever going to be one night, it should've been, but she wanted to make that decision herself, and not let it fall into the lap of the gods to decide for her.

Daniel was one of her oldest friends. He knew her probably better than Patrick did, and because of that, a massive void had developed in her world. She missed him too, and she was finding each day a struggle to keep calm and keep perspective on the important things.

She didn't need or want any distractions, with two young children to occupy, she was busy enough without the snivelling shameful Patrick following her around like a distressed puppy.

She missed Daniel too much to speak of. She had nobody to talk to, to ease her pain. She was alone as she knew Daniel had been, and she wished she could've been there for him more than she was. She wished her whole family had been there for him, to support him during his divorce and the investigation with the paper senior management.

She wished Patrick had been there for him, instead of his usual arrogant self. That was how she was now starting to see him, arrogant. He was self absorbed, determined to

253

have the world see things his way, and she hated herself for only now seeing him as his true self.

It frustrated her that it took him having an affair and the death of his brother, for her to see Patrick for the true man he really was. She wiped a tear from her face and wept as she realised she had married the wrong King.

Patrick knocked on the door, still wearing his suit from the funeral, and his tie was hanging loosely around his neck. It had been a tough and emotional day and he waited patiently for Helen to answer the door, at least then he could start to relax he thought, and move on.

He heard the locks being pulled back and the door opened.

She was beautiful, he thought, with her hair tussled down over her shoulders, wearing her casual clothing, and a glass of wine in her hand, she was adorable and appealing. He smiled at her, thankful for seeing a friendly face, and stepping towards her, she turned her cheek away from him.

"What are you doing here?" she asked.

Patrick stepped back. "I've left Georgina."

"So? Why did you do that?" her tone was direct, stern, unconcerned for his actions.

"Well – I thought, I thought we could -"

"Could what?" Helen asked. "What did you think would happen? Look Patrick, it was fun, to begin with, but that's all it was. Fun." She pulled the door close to her, closing the gap to stop him entering. "You should know how relationships within the police work. They're complicated, and it would be worse having your marriage break down because of an affair, and worse for me as I'd be the other woman. What would that do to my career prospects?"

"Career prospects?" Patrick asked, not believing what he was hearing. "This is about us."

"There is no *us*." Helen snapped. " I don't even think there was an *us*. It's over."

Patrick couldn't compute the revelation. He stood blankly on the door step, trying to think of something to say, something to make her know he wanted her. "I love you."

Helen took a sip from her glass and looked down at him. "Thanks. You were a good shag. Better than your brother."

Patrick shot her a look and was about to shout at her when the door was pulled open by someone.

"What's going on? I've opened another bottle of -" Superintendent Ian Withers said.

Patrick shot him a surprised look and then at Helen, who avoided his glare and turned to Withers. "I'll be back in a minute." She said, placing a tender hand on his chest to guide him back into the house.

Patrick gave a frustrated smile as his head allowed everything to fall into place. "Career prospects." He said quietly. "Danny was right, you used me. Who's next? The Chief Constable to make you the Assistant Chief?"

Helen shrugged, ignoring the tone of his comment. "Whatever the next step is, you'll have to call me ma'am." She said, and with nothing more, she closed the door on him.

For seconds Patrick stood alone on the doorstep, his rucksack in his hand. Slowly he turned and headed back to his car, throwing his bag on the back seat.

Behind the wheel he screwed up his face in frustration, and blinking back the tears he could feel his breathing and heart rate increasing.

What had gone wrong? He thought. He had it all so perfect. A wife, a mistress, a family. Why had everything conspired against him? He had done everything to his plan, he had thought of every contingency. *Why hadn't it all worked out? Why had nothing followed his plan?*

He banged his hand on the steering wheel and starting the engine, he gunned it. Revving it to the red line and with the wheels screeching on the wet road, he pulled the car out quickly and sped off down the road.

CHAPTER 28

"I would say you could do with a drink, but I think you've had enough already." James said, looking at the dishevelled shape of Patrick in front of him. "Have you driven like that?"

"Of course not." Patrick said, the effects of the alcohol burning a course through his body. "I may be drunk, but I still know the law."

"Where have you parked?"

Patrick thought for a moment and shook his head. "I have absolutely no idea." He looked at James, the despair in his face evident. "I need somewhere to stay."

James nodded and took his brothers arm. "You're always welcome."

In the parochial house, James and Patrick sat opposite each other. James knew that something had happened between him and Georgina, and he felt he should say something, but he refrained, and thought the best option was to let Patrick talk first, to allow him to lead the conversation.

They sat in silence for a moment, and James decided he couldn't wait any longer. "It was a good funeral."

"As good as funerals could be." Patrick said. "He wouldn't have liked all the attention."

"He would've preferred more drinking." James agreed.

"I know it feels different to other funerals because he was our brother," Patrick said, "but why does it feel *so* different?"

James had thought the same. He had conducted many funeral masses, and had overseen those of parishioners he had known for years, who could be called his friends, and it did feel different. "It was the way he died." He said. "It was the worst possible way."

"It feels – I don't know, almost personal." Patrick said. "With what happened to me, and then what happened to him, I don't know, it just feels so."

James flashed back to the confessional and how the mysterious man had made a specific reference to Patrick. *Was it really personal? Was it all a game to this man and James' family was at peril?*

Since that day he had debated whether he should tell Patrick or not about the confessions. He had spoken to his own Bishop about the moral dilemma regarding such a hypothetical situation, and his own moral code, his own vows, and the advice of the Bishop was to keep the sacred vow of confessional and not to divulge anything he hears.

But he could see the pain his brother was feeling. He was feeling it too. James was angry, frustrated, confused and boiling with rage that somebody could do something so cruel to his family, to his brothers.

When he had heard about the attack on Patrick he had quickly headed to the main altar in the church and knelt before the hanging crucifix and thanked God for protecting his brother. He had prayed that no other harm cam to his family, but when he received the news of Daniel, he had stood before the tortured statue of Christ.

"Quomodo tu, frater!" He had said in Latin.

"How dare you take my brother!"

"Sapientia et amore nihil feci filio nuntiet, quod reddis mihi?"

"I have done nothing but proclaim the wisdom and love of your Son, and this is how you repay me!?"

"Confessionis servavi te, et homo iste ambulat liber. Parce Domine, me autem fallo."

"I have protected the sacrament of Confession for you, and this man walks free. Forgive me Lord, but I must break my oath."

The following nights, James was plagued by nightmares, he couldn't sleep and his mind was restless with images of hell, purgatory, and damnation to the pit of discarded souls. He felt guilty and emotionally torn that he should've spoken in such a way to his God, and he prayed for forgiveness.

Now as he saw his brother, broken and beaten by the world and people he loved whom who he thought loved him back, James knew he had to make a decision.

"I think it was." James said quietly. "The way he spoke, sounded like it was personal."

Patrick rolled his head from side to side, trying to ease the stress in his neck, and he mulled over the words in his head. "What do you mean, *the way he spoke?*"

James took a breath, and he knew he couldn't turn back. "I've heard his confession." He said. "I've heard all of them, from the very first murder of the couple in the alleyway, he, whoever *he* is, has come to me for confession."

If ever there was a cure for drunkenness, that was it. Patrick was sat bolt upright, focused on his brother. "You gave him confession? You've seen him? The man who killed Danny? You know who he is?"

"No!" James said, "I've heard his voice. I've never seen him."

"But he's been here in the church!" Patrick snapped. "You could've called the police, called me! You could've stopped this before Danny was killed! Jesus Christ James-"

"PATRICK!" James snapped back. "This is not your police station, and this not your office. You do not speak that way in here or on these grounds."

"Oh, please forgive me," Patrick said sarcastically. "You seem to be doing that to anyone who comes in here, be it killer, murderer, or someone who swears. Why didn't you call me?"

"I couldn't!" James said.

Patrick was on his feet pacing around the room. He was agitated and frustrated, and his mind was trying to come to terms with the revelation that after all this time, after the murders there was a credible lead to follow. "Why couldn't you? Your fingers work don't they? You have my number? It hasn't changed, so there was no reason not to call me!"

James stood too and faced his brother. "I couldn't!"

"Give me a reason why?" Patrick said, the fury raging within him. He could've lashed out at James, but he resisted the urge to thrash him. "Why didn't you?" he shouted.

"You aren't the only one to swear an oath." James said.

Patrick was silent for a moment. "An oath?"

James could feel his hands shaking, and he tried to keep his voice calm. "You swore an oath to uphold the law of the land and to serve the Queen and Crown as a police officer. And I swore an oath to the church and to God to protect the faith and the blessed sacrament of confession. I cannot break the priest-penitent privilege."

"Then why are you telling me?" Patrick said. "Why are you telling me if you can't break it? Why dangle this crucial bit of information in front of me, and not be willing to do something about it?"

"I have thought about telling you for weeks," James said, "but I have never been able to bring myself to do it. All I'm telling you is that I've heard his confession. I'm not divulging *what* he said."

"I need to know!" Patrick demanded.

"I can't tell you!" James said, raising his own voice.

"Priest-Penitent privilege doesn't exist in English law." Patrick said. "I could drag you in front of court and you will be forced to divulge what you know."

"Then you'll be met by silence." James said. "Patrick I'm not messing around here. I will not tell you what he said, other than I have heard his voice."

"You have to tell me!"

"Here!" James said grabbing a small black book and throwing it at him. "The Bishops phone number is in there, speak to him. In fact," James paused and picked up his mobile phone and tossed it to Patrick. "Call Rome, call the Vatican, ask to speak to the Pope yourself and he'll tell you exactly the same as I've said. I'll even dial the number for you if you want!

"You have always been like this Paddy. Always laying your own beliefs onto others around you, you have always tried to make everyone see the world as you see it. Danny was right. You can't see the world through anyone else's eyes. This is my oath, my belief, my life, my job.

"You swore to protect the law, I swore to protect religion. I swear to protect the Church, and whatever you think of me, whatever twisted sense you think you have of being the righteous one of the family, I have the backing of a billion Catholics behind me who will support my actions for not breaking my vows.

"And for someone to try and dictate what vows I should break and uphold, coming from you who has broken his vow of marriage that you swore before God, is by no means pitiful, hypocritical, and downright obnoxious of you. How dare you try to direct my actions! You have no right to do that, not anymore!"

A silence fell on the room, and the only noise was the ticking clock on the mantel piece. It was rhythmic, steady, something for them both to focus on as they tried to calm down.

"James," Patrick said calmly, "I'm not berating your beliefs, your ideals, or your vows. I just need answers, and you're the one holding them."

"I can't tell you." James said again, exasperated.

"I've lost my wife, my family, my brother. I've lost the investigation, and most probably plans are being made for me to lose my job." Patrick said. "I need something, I need help to try and put right some of the crap that is going on in my life right now. I need to rebalance things. Call it karma."

"I'm a Catholic priest." James said quietly, and smiling. "I believe in the acts of God, rather than Karma."

Patrick smiled and sat back down on the chair. He ran his hands through his hair and looked up at his younger brother. "I'm sorry Jimmy. I really do understand what you're saying and I would never want you to undermine your oath. But you have to understand I am in a mire of crap at the moment and I need something to try and save everything from the brink of destruction."

James sat opposite him. "Thank you." He said. "And I know you're going through a rough patch. We all are." He looked at his brother, so similar he thought to how Daniel had been sitting there before Christmas. They were really too similar, he thought. "Maybe," James said, "there is a way to get this man, without me breaking my vows."

CHAPTER 29

Patrick sat in the chair in the parochial house and checked his phone again. He had sent text messages to Georgina apologising for his actions, but they had been met by silence. Since his arrival at the house a week before, he hadn't been outside. If he was honest, he didn't want to be outside, he didn't want to be a part of a world that turned on him.

He had spent most of his time in the spare room James had given him and he didn't know what to do with himself, with no work to go to, or family to be with. He had lay on his bed reading whatever book he could find, and had indulged his mind with *Divine Comedy*, an usual piece of work he thought, to find in a priests house.

He had helped with the maintenance of the church too, cleaning and fixing broken fixtures. Patrick could feel the stress of the last few weeks dissipate as he focused his mind on anything, other than his own problems. It was almost serene, he thought, to be helping in the church, listening to the organist practice, talking to the other helpers, and hearing the latest gossip.

As he lay on the bed, his mind wandered to the lady, Maureen, who came to the church each morning to clean. Patrick had found himself standing before the Sacred Heart chapel in the church when she stood next to him. He didn't realise she was there as he studied the statues, the carvings and the painted mural behind them.

"Amazing that they survived the fire." Maureen said.

Patrick suddenly notice she was there. "What fire?"

"16 years ago." She explained. "There was a fire here, started in this very spot. We don't know how it started, the fire brigade said it an electrical fault or something. Whatever it was, God was watching over us and he saved the church. Look," she pointed to the ceiling where it met the wall in the corner, "you can just make out the charring of the flames."

Patrick looked up at the corner and he could see the marks. As he turned to ask her another question Maureen had walked up onto the altar.

There was something about her that caught his attention. Her devotion to the church, so evident in her attending every day, her unassuming nature to not question who he was, and her simple joy of singing to herself as she almost singlehandedly vacuumed the church floor.

She may not have had much in the world, he thought, but she was happy.

Following the revelation of James hearing the murder's confession, both he and James had formulated a plan of action whereby a message would be sent to Patrick from James on his phone, telling him he was taking the killers confession again.

Patrick had questioned the purpose of such a message, stating if he was willing to text him, how come he wasn't willing to tell him about the content of the confession.

"I'll confess my deception later." James had said. "My soul will be clean."

Patrick hadn't been sure about the morality of his actions, but as long as he was willing to inform him should he hear another confession, then he was happy.

However, it did mean Patrick had to stay within the confines of the sterile and plain house. He couldn't risk leaving for any amount of time, should the killer attend confession.

Patience hadn't been one of his better qualities, but he tried to focus his mind as he waited for his phone to ring.

Each time over the previous days when James entered the confessional booth, his heart was pounding. He could feel the adrenaline in his body take hold of him, as he heard the muted shuffling of the next person seeking redemption. He could feel the palms of his hands begin to sweat but then, as they spoke, he let out a breath and relaxed as the parishioner began their confession.

James was just starting to calm his nerves when the voice was heard once more. *"Forgive me Father, for I have sinned."*.

Patrick was just starting to fall asleep, the effect of the book he was reading and the warmth of the house, combined with the serene peaceful environment where there was little noise and activity, he wearily looked at his phone.

There was a text message.

INFERNO

"Your sins are serious." James said, trying to control his anger as he listened to the man. "You killed my brother."

The man laughed. *"I thought I saw a familiarity. But he was guilty of Envy, he had sinned."*

"Show me a man who hasn't sinned." James said.

"Then all should be condemned." The man replied. *"These people do not seek the council, or the ear of God. They do not ask for his forgiveness, so they should, and will be, condemned by my hand. God has become a by-product of society. People will happily celebrate his birth, and will enjoy the materialistic trappings. They will take the good things of the Faith, but give nothing back throughout the year. Hypocrites."*

James looked down at his phone and saw the light flash as Patrick responded to his message. If only he could keep the man talking for a few more minutes, he thought.

Patrick headed through the adjoining corridor from the house to the sacristy at the side of the main altar. He emerged into the church, and found it to be dark, the lights were off.

There was nobody around and he walked slowly across the main aisle to the confessionals. He saw the curtains were drawn on the main centre cubicle, where James would be sitting, and the left hand curtain was also across.

Patrick could feel his heart begin to beat faster. After all the hard work, the investigation, the murders and death.

After all the turmoil and emotional upset he and his family had endured, now was the time to face the man responsible.

He pulled back the curtain, but was met with an empty booth. Patrick looked around him, trying to find anyone in the church, when from the central booth, he heard a moan.

He pulled the curtain across and saw James slumped in his seat with a bleeding cut across his temple. He stirred as Patrick tried to wake him.

"James," he whispered, knowing his voice would carry in the echoing vastness of the church. "Where is he? Where?"

James stirred and opened his eyes. "He must be still here." He said, "It just happened."

Patrick helped his brother to his feet and with his arm supporting James. "He must be here." He whispered, looking around him.

They slowly moved away from the confessionals, listening for any movement and trying to see any change in shape to the shadows.

James shrugged off his brothers arm telling him he was okay to walk. "I don't see him."

"He must be here." Patrick said, looking around.

He glanced over at James and saw the cut on his head, the blood dripping down the side of his face. He had a flash back to Daniel, seeing the body of his brother in the car park and the emotion started to fill him once more. Another member of his family had been attacked, that was all three of them now.

Was this a personal vendetta against them? Was Patrick the target? Was his whole family, Georgina, Clarissa, Charlie? He tried to think of who could possibly have that much hatred of him to act so cruelly to his family. He was a police officer, he had accepted the risks, but there was no need to bring his family into harm's way.

There was a flicker of a shadow near the altar and Patrick pulled James behind a stone pillar, grabbing his wrist. "There was something down there." He whispered.

As James pulled his arm free Patrick looked down and saw his wrist.

He stared at it, questions filling his mind, overloading his thoughts, and within a second he had computed the information and he spoke. "James," he said slowly, "when did Danny give you our father's watch?"

James was looking towards the altar, and looked up at his brother. A sly smile crept over his face and he laughed loud. "The night Danny died." He answered.

The sliver flash of the knife blade cut across Patrick's field of vision and he dodged the sharp edge at the last split second as he stepped away and tripped on the edge of a pew. "James!" Patrick shouted, seeing the knife in his brother's hand.

"James is gone." He replied. "I am Dante!"

CHAPTER 30

Patrick hit the wooden seat hard and stared up at his brother as he advanced on him, gleaming knife in hand. Hundreds of questions started flooding his mind as he watched James swing the knife in front of him.

"James!" Patrick shouted, kicking out at him as he took another step forward. "James stop!"

"I am Dante," James said, his voice hoarse, "messenger and the wielding hand of God, of true justice."

James lashed out at Patrick with the knife and slashed through Patricks trouser leg. Patrick shouted out in pain and instinctively reached up and pulled James toward him, bringing him off balance.

It had been a few years since his safety self defence training, but Patrick was starting to remember some of the key actions. *Bring the attacker closer to you, to limit their arc of attack.*

With a free elbow he jabbed it into James' shoulder and pushed down hard into the nerve point. James' shoulder fell away and the action gave Patrick a moment to scramble away from him. As he moved across the floor, he kicked out at James, catching him on the side of the knee, bringing him down to the floor.

Patrick hurried away from James, holding the wound on his leg. He was sweating and his heart was racing, and he tried to think of anything to do.

With a shaking hand, he pulled his mobile phone from his pocket and checked the screen, but swore under his breath as he saw he had no signal.

"You can't hide forever." James' voice echoed across the church. "You must face your own justice."

Patrick eased himself around the side of the stone column and looked out across the church. He saw the black shape of James on the other side, and ducked back from view.

"Everyone must face their justice." James said.

"Like Danny did? Like those other people you killed?" Patrick called out, hoping the echo would distort his location. He looked out again and saw James crossing the main altar and, with the shadows deep into the rear of the church, Patrick took a chance and hobbled to the next column.

"They were sinners." James called out. "They were sinners who lived in their own worlds of decadence, luxury, lust, and self pity. The lovers in the alley, lustful acts outside wedlock; the beggar, too lazy to get up and make something of himself. The couple who took me into their lives as their priest, their confessor. But they never saw the truth, how I despised their greed and need for more wealth. They had what was coming to them. The man who you tried to save, so full of his own gluttonous ways, a man who had never worked for anything in his life. None of them, they never searched out the desire to help others, they were only self absorbed in their own world."

"And Daniel?" Patrick replied. "And your own brother was what?"

"Guilty of envy. Jealousy. The green eyed demon burnt deep into his soul and was tearing him apart."

"Who? Who was he jealous of?" Patrick asked as he ducked down behind the last pew and scrambled across the floor to the centre aisle. He checked his phone again and begged it to pick up a signal.

"You, dear brother." James continued. "He was jealous of you and your life. As you were jealous of his all those years ago."

Patrick wasn't listening as he saw a signal bar appear on his phone. He dialled 999 and asked for police when the line was answered. "Detective Chief Inspector 7231 King," he said, "I need police assistance at St Martin's Church. ASAP. Offender has a knife, send armed response."

"We'll despatch them immediately." The operator said. *"Stay on the line."*

Patrick held the phone in his hand and looked out into the church, but he couldn't see James.

"He was jealous of you Paddy." James said. "Jealous of you for stealing his girlfriend, for stealing his dreams. He was the victim of your selfishness and blindness to his suffering for years, and it was unfortunate he became the victim again, but I released him from his pain, and now he sits with God."

Patrick felt himself sitting rigidly to the spot. He couldn't move. His mind was bombarded with memories, with images, with conversations he had had with Daniel over the years. The comments he made, the looks he gave, they were all starting to make sense.

"And the others?" Patrick asked, looking out down the central aisle.

"They knew their sins!" James said, his face appearing from the pew in front of Patrick. The knife swung down and cut across Patrick's outstretched hand. He shouted in pain and fell backwards landing hard on the tiled floor and releasing his grip on the phone, sending it scattering across the floor.

"And what about me?" Patrick asked. "You attacked me once, why did I live? Why!?"

"You weren't part of the plan," James answered. "Until now."

James moved quickly and advanced on Patrick as he scrambled away and avoided the slashes. Patrick pulled himself up and hobbled away from James who slowly followed him down the central aisle towards the altar.

"It's your destiny brother." James called out. "No escaping it. Others have met their demise through their sins – Lust, Sloth, Greed, Gluttony, Envy, and soon there will be Pride and Wrath."

"Why are you doing this?" Patrick asked. "What made you become like this?"

James stopped his advancement and looked at his brother as he tripped up the altar steps. "Nothing made me like this," he said, "I've always been this way." He walked forward slowly, watching Patrick try to move away. "I learnt very quickly how to hide my symptoms from you all. From you, from Danny, from our parents. Hospital helped, and I'll admit the drugs did too. But it was at the Abbey that I found myself. I was taught self control, self-discipline, and I soon gave up the little pills that so numbed my mind and confused my soul. I was taught to be able to control my emotions through prayer and inner-contemplation. The voice of God within me focused my mind, and calmed my nerves.

"The church gave me more than faith. It gave me a path to follow and a way of coping." He stopped at the bottom of the steps. "But there is only so much pretence you can give. So I occasionally let the other side of myself loose to indulge in this passion I have for inflicting God's judgement on people.

"There was the small matter of absolving myself of my sins, and after the first death by my hands, when I was in Wales, I confessed my sins to the priest at the local church. But then I knew he would've gone straight to the police so he unfortunately became number two."

Patrick was lay on the stairs to the altar, listening. His leg throbbed with pain, the blood seeped though fingers as he gripped at the deep wound. He knew there was no way he could bear any weight on it. He listened to James talk and remembered the news coverage of the murder of the priest 6 years before. "That was you?"

James nodded. "It was indeed. But we're wasting time, justice awaits you brother."

Patrick was taken by surprise by the speed in which James lunged at him. He tried to grab the knife hand, but he couldn't get a good enough grip to properly disarm him. James was on top of him, thrashing about, elbowing, punching and hitting Patrick whenever he could.

The knife sailed down and sliced through Patricks coat. They wrestled on the steps and Patrick could feel them losing balance a second before they both rolled off and down the steps to the main floor.

Patrick hit the floor hard with James on top of him, he looked up to see the fierce, wild like eyes staring down at him.

Suddenly, James coughed and spluttered. His movements became weak and he rolled off Patrick.

He looked down at James and saw protruding from his chest, his own knife. He coughed again and blood spurted out of his mouth.

"James?!" Patrick shouted. "James!". He pulled his brother close to him, holding him in his arms. "Jesus, what have you done?"

James smiled. "Don't use his name in vain!"

"I'll get an ambulance. Don't worry." Patrick said. He was about to move off just as James' bloodied hand reached up and grabbed his arm.

"Stay." He said, his voice quieter. "Stay and sit with me."

Tears were running down Patrick's face and he rubbed his cheeks with his own wounded hand, smearing his face. "You can't die!" he said. "You're all I have left."

James smiled weakly and pulled his brother's head down to his, "Wrath and Pride." He said. "You killed me with Wrath and Pride."

CHAPTER 31

One Month Later...

Detective Chief Inspector Patrick King stood before the security man, and showing his police identification, he was passed through the metal detector. He headed up the stairs to the 1st floor and was met by Superintendent Withers. They shook hands and Withers took him towards a large rotund man, the barrister for the court case, Derek Slater, QC.

"Inspector King," Slater said, "how are you doing?"

"Fine." He answered simply.

There was an uncomfortable silence between them and Patrick didn't excuse himself as he walked away and sat down.

He had spent the previous day in the witness stand in Crown Court number 3, giving his evidence in the case of what had been nicknamed *The Deadly Sin Murders* by some arms of the press.

He had been required to explain and detail his actions during and after the investigation, and the subsequent events in the church with James. He had found it difficult to recall, recount, and justify his actions within the church, and each second he was in the witness box, was like he was living the day over and over.

He wasn't even sure if he was recalling it correctly. He remembered the words James had spoken, and he knew he had shouted out for help to the empty church. If he was as religious or devout to his faith as his bleeding brother in his arms, he would've sworn that God must've heard his cries for help, for as he shouted the church doors were opened and armed police officers entered, guns raised, shouting orders.

Patrick shouted back at them to get help, but they still pointed their guns at him and James. Patrick had to waste precious seconds explaining he was an officer himself, and finally a call was made for an ambulance to attend.

The armed officers had been trained to deal with emergency first aid incidents and they quickly began to assess and work on James' wound. Patrick was pulled away from his bleeding brother and questions were directed at him.

Was he hurt?
What had happened?
Was there anyone else around?
Who is he?
Where was the weapon?

Patrick tried to answer the questions as best he could, but it was a frantic few moments as more police officers arrived and Patrick was escorted away from the church. He was driven back to the police station and taken to one of the familiar interview rooms and left on his own.

He remembered imagining the activity that would be surrounding the church. James would've been taken by ambulance to the hospital, under constant guard by armed officers. The church and the parochial house would be sealed off as crime scenes and no doubt Michael Ferguson and his team would be dispatched to examine it.

The CID phones would be ringing and conversations would be whispered about his brother, and, if Patrick had known anything all along.

He couldn't do anything, there was nothing he could do except sit and wait for someone to either interview him or find out more details. He honestly couldn't remember how long he was there, but he recalled using the time to try and make sense of what had happened.

His mind recounted the evidence from the previous murders as best as it could, and then rearranged it into some sort of coherent workable theory. He tried to see the lines of clarity between the apparent randomness of the murders and the clues left behind.

He shook his head as he remembered the name James had called himself, *Dante*. The name he had used when he had mental disparity episodes previously when he was younger. Dante, the Italian poet and author of *Divine Comedy* and descriptor of the seven deadly sins, Lust, Greed, Gluttony, Wrath, Envy, Sloth, and Pride.

It couldn't have been a coincidence, Patrick thought that James would fashion his actions on the deadly sins *and* call himself Dante? It must've been planned. But why hadn't he seen it before? Was he blinded by brotherly love and loyalty? Was he subconsciously covering up his brothers actions?

Or was it that at the time there was no reason to think his brother was involved? Patrick had to force himself to believe the latter, it was the only reasoning that was true, despite the accusations defence barristers would throw at him.

But the more he sat and thought about it, the more things made sense. James' position as a priest allowed him a certain shroud of protection against suspicion. Walking the alleyways through the lines of homeless people like Leo, wouldn't draw attention as he often helped out at shelters and would've been almost welcomed amongst them.

But likewise, working within the church he would've befriended more wealthy and affluent people. Clive and Jess Lancashire were Christians, and helped charities when they could, all to off-set the image others had of them as rich upper class toffs. *Greed.*

Calum Book, Patrick thought, was where it started to become a bit more personal for James. He remembered how he had sat with James and discussed Calum Book's role in ending Daniels career. It was a personal revenge attack, he could see it now. It was James getting back at Calum Book for hurting his brother, but he had cleverly used it as an underlying objective, hidden by the more pronounced reasoning of *Gluttony.*

The couple in the alleyway. *Lust.* They must've been strangers to him, Patrick thought. There was no other link he could think of between him and Caroline Richards and Adrian Leyton.

And then that left Daniel. *Envy.* His own brother. What would drive a man to murder his own brother, he didn't know. Perhaps interviews with therapists and doctors would reveal why he did that.

If he survived life imprisonment.

Patrick held his head and tried to remember a prayer he could say that would allow his brother to survive. He was torn between wanting justice for the murders committed and not seeing his brother die. He couldn't bury another brother, he knew he wouldn't be able to cope with the loss.

As he thought about the prospect of losing another brother, the door opened and Superintendent Withers entered, followed by Helen Kolar.

He looked at them both, remembering the moment he had discovered their affair. He wanted to make a small jibe at them, but in the given situation, he knew it wasn't wise. "How is he?" Patrick asked.

Withers sat down and handed Patrick a coffee. "He'll live." He said. "There was extensive blood loss, but the ambulance and doctors managed to keep him going."

Patrick hung his head in relief. His brother was alive. He could feel the emotion building up within him, he wanted to shout out in delight, and as he looked up, with a smile starting to form on his face, Withers' stern look brought him back to the grave reality of the situation.

"I need you to talk us through exactly what happened there." Withers said. "We need to bring this case to a close."

Patrick wanted to argue with them, he wanted to shout at them and tell them to leave him alone, but he couldn't. He knew that the career hungry Helen Kolar would try to manipulate everything so that she could tell her superiors of her sterling and excellent team leading abilities. And it was these that led to the capture of the killer. With Withers by her side, Patrick thought, there would be no doubt she would be rewarded for it. They just needed to know his story so they could fit their own around it.

Patrick looked at them both in the eye. He didn't want to relive the events, but he had to. He took a deep breath and recounted the events at the church.

His time in the box was unnerving as he explained his actions to the court. He was cross examined by the defence barrister and questioned once more by the prosecution, and finally, after a total of 8 hours in the witness box, he was released from the court.

Withers and Kolar were waiting outside the court as he emerged and they both approached him. "How was it?" Withers asked.

"Fine." Patrick said.

"Good, well hopefully that will be enough to satisfy the jury."

Patrick turned to Withers and looked at him hard. "That's my brother in the dock. Do not discard him like any other criminal."

"Excuse me, Inspector." Withers said, "but he is a multiple murderer. He deserves to be sent down for a hanging."

Patrick couldn't help himself and his fist struck Withers hard in the chest, winding him, sending him to his knees. Helen Kolar pushed Patrick away, and other officers in attendance rushed over and pulled him back.

"Don't think you can use this to further your career. Either of you." Patrick said, his voice carrying and echoing around them. "He is my brother and I'll be more loyal to him than to this job."

Slowly Withers stood up. "What job?" he said. "You'll be fired before the sun goes down."

Patrick smiled at him. "Beat you to it. The Chief Constable had my resignation letter this morning, along with copies of Daniel's computer records stating and revealing Helen Kolar as his source within the force."

Withers stopped and looked at her. "What?"

"My brother was a careful man." Patrick said. "Emails, phone calls, phone records, he even taped some of your more private conversations where you revealed more information than you should have. But that was the point wasn't it? You feed him information to keep him happy, and then you think he's in your pocket when the papers print something you don't like. Why did you do that?" he asked her. "To show senior management you had contacts and could work the press? To put yourself in a better light to get another promotion? That fell apart though didn't it when the senior officers took a more proactive official response rather than what you were planning for, a more subversive underhand deal. And when they started attacking Daniel, you ditched him and cut all contact."

"You can't prove that." Helen said.

Patrick shrugged. "Not my problem now, the Chief Constable has all the papers, it's his decision."

Patrick smiled to himself as the revelation hit home with Withers. He stepped up to him and talked close to his ear. "You dragged my name and my brother's through the mud. She's shagging you to get ahead in her career, and Professional Standards will be in touch soon to investigate you both. Through her, you're now poisoned. Enjoy your time together."

Patrick walked past Withers and headed back downstairs and out into the fresh air. He didn't know if he should've reported the misconduct of Withers and Kolar, but he had reasoned it was what Daniel would've done, and in his honour and in his memory, he followed his brother's morals.

As he approached his car he saw someone standing next to it, and getting closer he saw Georgina waiting for him. They hadn't spoken much since the incident at the church, and he had to admit that his mind wasn't in the best place to try and work out their problems. He wanted to get back with her, he wanted to be a family again, but he knew it would be an uphill battle to regain her trust.

"Hi." He said simply.

"How was court?" she asked.

Patrick shrugged. "It was fine, considering."

"How's James?"

Patrick leaned against the car next to her. "I don't know. I'm not allowed to make contact. But seeing him in court, he looks fine."

Georgina looked at her husband and she could see how the events of the previous months had aged him. There was something different about him, she thought. It was as though he was losing the battle against a world that was fighting him from every angle. "You had a job to do." She said. "Your morality and ethos and dedication to what you believe in is one of the reasons I fell in love with you. You would never had overlooked James' actions, and I think he knew it. He showed you who he really was because he knew he couldn't keep it hidden forever."

Patrick looked at her. "Are you saying I've done the best thing for him? To have him sent to prison?"

Georgina reached out and held his hand. "I'm saying you did the right thing for the good of yourself." She looked at him, "Come on, the kids are waiting for you."

EPILOGUE

The classical music stirred through the thick stone walls and heavy steel doors. The prisoners were all sealed within their cells, some lying on their beds, others reading, some were watching TV, but all could hear the melody of the orchestra call out from Cell 34B.

James King stood before the barred window and looked at the starry night in the heavens above. The music wrapped around him as he listened to the tune play from his stereo.

On the lower bunk bed lay the body of his cellmate. Dead, choked by a bed sheet being wrapped around his neck. The man hadn't struggled much, but being taken by surprise, he wouldn't have, James thought. On a piece of paper, lying on the chest of the dead man was written one word: *Wrath*.

Like the music playing around him, his mission for God was meant to be a masterpiece, but his brother had disrupted it. How dare he? He thought.

James wasn't angry at being caught, tried and convicted of his crimes, but more angry at not being allowed to complete his mission.

But, he had been loyal to God's word, and during a dream he had been visited by a vision from heaven who told him to continue his quest, to satisfy the Lord.

His cellmate had suffered because of the message, and James was relieved the end was near.

He turned from the window and pulled the hood of his prison issue jacket over his head like a cowl. He took the twisted bed sheet that was fed through the bars of the window and wrapped it around his neck.

James crossed himself. "Bless me Father, for I have sinned." he said as he fell to the floor, allowing the sheet to pull tight around his neck, compressing on the arteries and veins in his neck.

He focused his mind to resist the urge to stand up.

A few more seconds, he thought, and then the noose would become too tight to even pull off.

He could feel his vision blurring, his ears were ringing and he was gasping for breath.

Not long before he would be reunited with his God, he thought. And in the remaining seconds of his life, James King looked at the note in his hand, one word on a single piece of paper. He had accomplished his mission, and only one word could describe it: *Pride.*

The End

THREE KINGS

ABOUT THE AUTHOR

David Whelan is a new British writer based in
Worcestershire. He has written screenplays,
short stories, and poems
Currently working as a Forensic Scene Investigator for
West Midlands Police, he has an extensive knowledge of
forensic practices and techniques.
He lives in Bromsgrove, Worcestershire with his wife
Alison, and son, Joshua.

http://birmingham-writer.blogspot.co.uk/
On Facebook: **David Whelan – The Writer**

Other Books by the same author:
Chimera
Dragon's Theatre
The Last Vatican Knight
Through the Lens
The Fox Norton Adventures: Volume One

For Children:
The Story of…: (Vol. 1)

CHIMERA
David Whelan

DRAGON'S THEATRE
David Whelan

THE LAST VATICAN KNIGHT
David Whelan

THROUGH THE LENS
David Whelan

The Fox Norton Adventures: Volume One

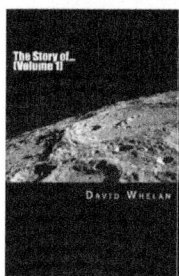

DAVID WHELAN

THREE KINGS

DAVID WHELAN

Printed in Great Britain
by Amazon